the People's Republic

Stories of Boulder, Colorado

by Rob Sheely

Illustrations by Mike Keefe

Boulder Weekly Press, Boulder, Colorado

First Boulder Weekly Press Edition 2003
Copyright © 2003 by Robert L. Sheely
All rights reserved.

Published by:
Boulder Weekly Press
690 South Lashley Lane
Boulder, CO 80305
303.494.5511
www.boulderweekly.com

ISBN 0-9747100-0-8

Dedication

For Annette, the best ally and supporter any writer, and any husband, could ask for. And for Amber who has made her way into many of these stories as magically as she has come into our life. And of course for Mom and Dad who still don't understand why anyone would want to write for a living, but who have always loved and supported me anyway.

Acknowledgments

Big thanks to:

Pamela White for her invaluable friendship, support and advice. No one else looks after their writers better.

Sue France for all her painstaking work under inhuman pressure.

Kristin Overn for her last-minute proof reading help, and also for being my longest writing friend — as well as friend in general. All the years and adventures we have shared!

Mike Keefe who stepped in and did wonderful work under tight deadline.

Vince Darcangelo for his cheerful support and week-by-week attention to each story as it comes from my computer to his desk.

Wayne Laugeson for his unwavering support.

Susan Newsome and the Boulder Bookstore for giving The People's Republic a public reading long before there were enough stories to make up a book.

Pete Miller for his week-to-week attention to the stories.

Damien DeLeon for his advise and encouragement.

A special thanks for Stewart Sallo who took a chance on the first fiction column in the Weekly's history and who is now taking a chance on the first book in the Weekly's history. I only hope to do his faith proud.

Contents

Forward

I grew up in the shadow of the Flatirons and have lived in Boulder almost all of my life. The town has changed a lot since the college students who lived across from me painted Richard Nixon's face on the hood of an old car — and then bashed the car to bits with baseball bats. That was spring of 1974, and I was 10.

Boulder has always been characterized by the energy, creativity and outspokenness of its residents. People here have never been afraid to try things — exotic foods, new religions, sexual positions, alternative lifestyles, illicit drugs. And most are pretty tolerant of other people's choices.

Still, the town has changed since it first earned the sobriquet "The People's Republic." The house I grew up in, which my parents bought for $25,000, is now worth almost $400,000. Riots over the Vietnam War have given way to riots over beer and football. And the laid-back pot-smoking hippy of the early 1970s has been all but replaced by the laid-back pot-smoking yuppy. Yet Boulder remains a town where anything can happen — and usually does.

I'd like to say I had the vision to bring Rob on board, but I didn't. Wayne Laugesen was editor at the time and, after reading a few sample columns, he decided the column was a perfect fit for the paper. Although I, too, am an author of fiction, it wasn't until I read Rob's column myself that I understood exactly what he was trying to do — and how well he was doing it.

Using masterfully drawn characters and an economy of words, Rob was telling the truth about our town. Like a political cartoonist who gets nearer to the heart of things with a handful of words and a picture, Rob was using the power of fiction to put Boulder and its people under the microscope. It's short-story-meets-caricature — funny, poignant, always smart and salient.

More than a year has passed since People's Republic joined the Arts & Entertainment section of Boulder Weekly. Since then, it has consistently been a reader favorite. We're certain people who love Boulder — and those who hate it — will find plenty between these covers to make them laugh, cringe and nod their heads. It's the Boulder you know and love — and a Boulder you've never seen before.

Enjoy!

Pamela White

Pamela White
Editor, Boulder Weekly
Author, *Sweet Release* and *Carnal Gift*

The cheapest house in Boulder

When Jill's Grammy died and left her $20,000, Tom urged her to start a Roth IRA. Jill test drove a Miata. Tom brought home mutual fund prospectuses. Jill brought home travel brochures. Tom lectured her about responsibility. Jill politely suggested he "get off my ass." Just when things were about to boil over, they turned to each other and said one word:

"Boulder."

The next Sunday, they were standing, shell-shocked, in the entry of a 900-square-foot carriage house, offered at $399,900, when Jack, the listing agent, came over.

"New to the Boulder market?"

"We live in Westminster," said Tom.

"We rent in Westminster," said Jill. "We both work in Boulder. We eat in Boulder. We hike in Boulder. We work out in Boulder. We *belong* in Boulder."

Jack handed them a card. "Jeff's a mortgage broker. He works miracles."

They went to see Jeff. He crunched the numbers. After 10 minutes he said, "Have you considered a condo?" After 20, "Have you considered Rock Creek?"

Tom's cell phone rang. It was Jack. "Something just popped up on the MLS. A former rental. Meet me there."

They flew up 36, off the ramp, and west on Table Mesa to Moorhead. A quick right, up a couple blocks, and they were there.

3

"Hurry," said Jack.

Tom and Jill ran inside. It was tiny. The appliances were avocado. The carpet smelled of beer and cat. The bedrooms were cells. The backyard was a moonscape. Just beyond thundered four lanes of semis, SUVs and Harleys. Scrawled on the fence was "I Felta Delta!"

Tom looked at Jill. Jill looked at Tom. They both looked at Jack.

"We'll take it."

The morning of the closing, Tom and Jill drove into Boulder an hour early. There was a homeless guy at the bottom of the ramp. On a whim, Jill leaned over Tom and rolled down his window.

"What are you doing?" hissed Tom as Jill took out a 20. "He'll only use it to get high."

"God bless you, ma'am," said the homeless guy, his eyes widening.

"I feel pretty high myself right now," said Jill. "Don't you?"

Tom couldn't bring himself to be mad with her. Not today. They headed to the title company. In the lobby, the closer came out and introduced herself as Candy. "There's a teensy problem," she said.

"What is it?" said Tom.

"The balance confirmation on your cash reserves came back $218 short."

"That can't be," said Tom. "I made sure we had exactly what you told me to have in the bank."

"The original papers I faxed you didn't include the mortgage insurance."

"So it's *your* mistake," said Jill.

Candy smiled sweetly. "We can reschedule for later in the week. Unless you can bring me back a deposit slip for $218 — "

"We'll do it. Don't reschedule!"

In the car, Tom and Jill totaled up the contents of his wallet and her purse: $85.12.

In minutes, they were pulling into a parking lot. "'Savers'?" said Jill.

Inside, Tom asked for the clothes buyer. He was directed to "Conchata," a woman in a blue apron.

"How much for my shoes?" Tom said. Conchata cast an experienced eye at the nearly new loafers. "I can give you 20."

"Done. How much for my belt?"

In just under nine minutes, Tom and Jill traded every piece of clothing for $113 in cash, plus replacement outfits grabbed off the nearest racks.

"We're $19.88 short," said Tom. Jill grabbed the keys from him. In less than a minute they were racing east on Table Mesa toward the on-ramp from 36. Tom stared at Jill in disbelief.

"I gave him that 20 because he needed it. Well, now, I need it back." Jill pulled off into the PDQ parking lot just past the ramp. The now-empty ramp.

Jill opened the door, jumped out and headed over to the ramp. Tom buried his face in his hands, but not before an image of unforgettable horror burned itself into his visual cortex: Jill, in a shapeless faded dress and red high-top sneakers, bending down to accept a folded bill from a matron in a Chevy Suburban.

Three weeks later Tom lay awake in the darkness of their new bedroom. Jill's gentle breathing rose and fell beside him. The sticky-sour aftertaste of cheap champagne lingered in the back of his throat, along with a persistent note of beer and cat. Through the open window a motorcycle Doppler-screamed its way down 36. Tom closed his eyes and let his head sink into the pillow.

"I'm the luckiest man in the world," he thought.

Flying a sign

Benny blew into town in the back of a Ford pickup. He'd tried to hop in the front when the guy pulled over, just outside of Topeka. But the driver got one whiff and said, "In the back." Benny didn't mind. He had a bottle.

It was dark when the guy banged on the back of the cab, waking Benny from a drunken half-sleep. He waved thanks and jumped out. If he could believe the sign, he was on a street named "Baseline." The baseline for what, he wondered.

He counted a Taco Bell, a McDonalds, a Denny's and several other names he didn't recognize. Benny checked his money pocket. Empty. Looked like it was dumpster diving on the menu tonight.

An hour later, his stomach filled with the remains of other people's happy meals, Benny ambled past a couple of tall buildings into an open field. He spread out the ratty wool blanket that was his prize possession, and bundled up for the night. He stared up at the stars and drained the last inch of apricot schnapps into his grateful mouth.

Say what you will about being a drunk; it simplifies your life. When Benny awoke the next morning, there was only one action item for the day: get booze.

That meant getting money. Benny didn't know anyone here to borrow from and he was no good at stealing. That left begging. He rummaged through his knapsack. "Disabled Vet" was the old classic, but someone had stolen his prop crutch. "Why Lie? Want Beer" had been good for a nice little run, but its

7

time had passed. "Hungry" was direct, but it invited food instead of money. In the end he decided on a bit of whimsy: "Born under a Bad Sign. Need a New One."

He walked until he came to a road called "Table Mesa." Was that supposed to be a joke? He followed it to the bottom of a highway off ramp. Out came the sign and he was in business.

The first dozen cars or so ignored Benny, the drivers staring straight ahead like zombies. He remained at his post, and eventually a car pulled up and rolled down its window.

"God bless you," Benny said automatically. But, instead of a bill, the middle-aged woman handed him a pamphlet for the local homeless shelter.

A couple of cars later, Benny got another rolled-down window. College boys, by the look of them, in a cherry red Camaro. An alarm went off in Benny's head, but too late. The driver spat a big gob right in his face.

"Get a job!" The college boys drove off, hooting with laughter.

Before Benny could even wipe his face on his sleeve, a tan Corolla pulled up. The driver ignored him, but the passenger, a cute little blonde, leaned over and rolled down the driver's side window.

"God bless you," said Benny, taking a bill from her hand. Holy Mother of God, it was a 20!

Benny looked up, searching for any witnesses to his outrageous good fortune. Bums were like sharks; they could smell a twenty from miles away. He slid the bill casually into his money pocket, picked up his knapsack and sauntered away. There was a liquor store by the corner PDQ, but it wouldn't open for awhile. Benny found a spot in the shade.

Oh, man. 20 bucks and it wasn't even eight in the morning! He luxuriated in planning how to spend his windfall. First, of course, he'd score some booze. And not the cheap stuff. Something nice that would go down smooth.

Screw that. Instead, he'd get two bottles of the cheap stuff.

Or maybe three. With the left-over money, he'd get a real meal. Or maybe some shoes from the Salvation Army. Or some pants. Shit, maybe even a new wool blanket.

Then the strangest thought hit Benny. Maybe it was because he had achieved his action item so early in the day. Or maybe it was the memory of the cute little blonde in the Corolla. Whatever the reason, Benny asked himself, "Why not go straight?"

Whoa! Where did that come from? But the thought wouldn't go away. Why couldn't it be Benny driving that Corolla? Why not him glaring at the blonde as she gave their hard-earned cash to some dirty bum?

"I'll tell you why," said another part of Benny's brain. "You're a drunk. You get the shakes if you go half a day without booze."

"I'll go to detox and get clean."

"Okay, but can you stay clean?"

"Why not? According to this pamphlet, they'll give me housing. They'll get me in a 12-step group. They'll find me a job."

As he thought these words, Benny actually saw himself doing it. He saw himself making it though the day without poisoning his body. He saw himself exercising. Boulder was supposed to be a healthy place, right? Everybody works out, runs, roller blades. Why not Benny?

Sure it would be hard to turn his life around. It would take every ounce of personal strength he could muster. But what was the alternative? How much longer could he go on like this before he found himself face down in some alley, puking up his very life?

Benny glanced over at the liquor store in time to see a guy walk up and unlock the door.

Finally, he thought, picking up his knapsack and heading in to get something to drive these crazy thoughts out of his head.

Word

Jason backed the Saturn out of the driveway. Mrs. Collier next door looked up from her pansies to give him a little wave. He ignored her, slipping on his shades.

He shifted into forward, wishing for the thousandth time his mother hadn't insisted on buying an automatic. At the end of the block, he slid a CD from his knapsack into the player and jacked up the volume until the car rocked on its patented four-wheel independent suspension. Finally, he pulled his stocking cap down over his forehead.

The transformation was complete.

Notorious J slipped into traffic, cruising like a shark in a school of whitefish. He relished the way their heads swiveled when he slid alongside or pulled up behind them at a light.

"Thass right," he whispered to himself. "N— in the house." He repeated the word out loud. Letting it roll around in his mouth like dark molasses. To his mother it was the absolute worst word a person could say. She taught multicultural studies at the University. She believed in diversity and tolerance.

He shook his head. What kind of shit was that? Maybe her pet Negro people of Afro-American color were content to be "tolerated," but a real N— don't take that shit. Especially not off some middle-class, oh so righteous, lily white teacher lady.

He glanced at the dashboard clock. Time to spare before she expected him home from his "errand." He turned onto Broadway.

Notorious J circled the streets in the gathering dusk, looking for a parking place where none of his mother's colleagues were likely to spot the car. The last thing he needed was his mother knocking on his bedroom door to say, "Ms. Nosy-Ass said she saw the Saturn parked on the Hill last night."

He found a spot between a Cherokee and a Corolla and nosed in, scraping the Corolla's bumper. He looked around, hoping no one saw. The street was empty. Good. He climbed out.

"Smooth move, jerk-off!" a voice called down from an upper window of a nearby frat house. Notorious J winced. He thought about shooting the asshole a bird, but decided to play it cool and walk away.

He turned the corner onto 13th Street and joined the flow of pedestrian traffic. He moved slow, careful not to catch the eye of any of the college students. Across the street he recognized Samantha from fifth period English with her pathetic blonde dreadlocks. Who did she think she was fooling?

He reached his destination, Albums on the Hill. He walked inside and found the rap section. The rest of the world disappeared.

One by one he flipped through the black faces with their attitude, their cool, their challenge to everything the so-called "majority culture" stood for. He imagined his mother in front of a classroom full of just these faces.

He knew just what she'd say. How many times had he heard the lecture? About how the dominant culture imposed a sense of internal oppression upon the weakest members of society, leading them to disrespect women, to disrespect their own culture, to disrespect themselves.

Disrespect.

She got that much right. Who the hell did she think she was fooling anyway? If she loved "diversity" so much, why was she living here in Uncolorado?

Notorious J checked his watch. Shit, time to book. He reluctantly pulled his hands away from the CDs and turned to go. He bumped into an aging hippie in a denim jacket.

"Careful there, little dude."

"Sorry," he mumbled, wishing for the thousandth time that he had a crew to back him in front of fools like these.

On the way back up 13th, he scoped out the sidewalk in front of him. And there he saw it. Up ahead in the sea of white faces. An island of blackness.

Three Brothers walking together. Talking. Chilling. Keeping it real.

He pulled his eyes down. Don't stare. A quick flick back up. There they were. Coming his way.

Be cool. Just be cool.

He let his arms relax. He slowed his stride. His head bobbed ever so slightly.

Another quick glance and then away. Be cool. Do not act the fool.

Another glance. Half a block and closing.

He forced himself to take a deep breath.

Twenty feet ahead.

Ten.

Five.

They moved abreast of him and he gave them a little nod. The closest one gave him a nod in return. He was certain.

He felt a warmth fill his chest. Then out came the words that he would regret for the rest of his life.

"Whassup, N—?"

The three black guys stopped in their tracks. Jason froze, his mouth hanging open as if straining to somehow suck the word back in.

No one moved until he tore himself away and ran as fast as he had ever run, his breath coming like daggers in his throat. Just another 16-year-old kid. As small and naked and white as anyone had ever, ever been.

A day of firsts

Tom awoke on their first morning in Boulder with a list of chores to be accomplished. Jill took it and tore it in half.

"What's the idea?" he said.

"We can't waste our first day on chores. There are too many important things to do."

"Like what?"

"Come on!" She grabbed the car keys and pushed him out the door.

"Just exactly where are we going, Jill?" Tom glared at her from the passenger seat.

"Up," she said, following Baseline west until it climbed Flagstaff Mountain. She pulled off at the overlook and into the first open parking spot. She grabbed Tom's hand and dragged him over to the railing.

"I think I see our house!" she said, pointing.

"Yes," he said. "It's the one that needs painting and mowing and trimming..."

She rolled her eyes. He ignored her. Next she drove to McGuckin Hardware, again dragging a reluctant Tom inside. They were immediately surrounded by green vests.

"Name one thing you've always, always wanted," she said.

"Well," he said, "I suppose we could use an extra drop cloth for painting the living room."

After much arm twisting he relented and bought himself a 12" sliding compound mitre saw. Back in the car, Jill turned onto Arapahoe, only to find herself stuck at some road work by the University.

"Oh, goody," said Tom. "Our first Boulder traffic jam."

"That's the spirit," laughed Jill. Tom crossed his arms and sighed.

Finally, they crossed Broadway. Jill passed the Wild Oats and hung a right into the big parking lot. She threw open her door and ran onto the grass.

"Take off your shoes," she said, hopping out of hers. "Come on, Tom. You can pout tomorrow. Today we're going wading in Boulder Creek!"

Jill stood knee-deep in the icy water, hooting for joy. Tom waded in up to his ankles.

"I can't feel my feet," he said.

"How about brunch on the Mall?" Jill said as they were putting back on their sock and shoes.

"How about going home and acting like adults?"

She stuck out her tongue and dragged him over the bridge and toward downtown. On the Mall, she breathed in the flowers, the crowds, the music, the panhandlers, the sculpture, the shops, the restaurants, the whole joyous melange. Tom breathed in some pollen and exploded in a fit of sneezing.

A woman stopped them and asked if they were locals, and they made their first apology for living in Boulder.

"We got lucky," said Tom.

"If my Grammy hadn't died unexpectedly..." said Jill.

"I just wanted directions to the Farmer's Market," said the woman.

They were watching the children scrambling on the rocks in front of Smith's Shoes when Jill asked Tom where he wanted to eat.

"I've got a coupon for Applebee's," he said.

She hit his shoulder hard. "We live in Boulder now. We don't patronize national chains."

"That's it," he said, turning on her. "Give me the keys. I'm going home and getting started painting the living room."

"While you're at it," she said. "don't forget to paint the stick up your ass."

Before they knew it they were thick into their first fight as Boulderites. Tom stomped off East. Jill stomped off West. Like participants in an out-sized duel, they continued until they reached opposite ends of the Mall and turned around. Each was surprised not to see the other.

"Well," thought each, "I'm not going to be the one to apologize."

They each paced up and down at their chosen end of the Mall, waiting for the other to come begging. When this didn't happen, a sense of panic began to set in. Slowly, each began to drift back toward the center of the Mall. Step by step, they drew closer until they stood across from each other on opposite sides of Broadway.

The light changed and the Red Digital Readout started counting down. Each stood, waiting for the other to cross. The Readout hit zero and the light changed. Traffic streamed between them, but their eyes remained locked on one another. The light changed again. Still they did not move.

"10," said the Red Digital Readout. "9, 8, 7, 6, 5 — "

Their wills crumpled at the same time and they ran into the street, meeting on the double yellow line. They were kissing when the light changed, and their whispered apologies were drowned out by horns honking and bystanders applauding.

They strolled hand in hand not talking. Jill pulled Tom to a stop and laid her face against his chest.

"I apologize for bulldozing you," she said. "I just wanted our first day to be special. I wanted to rack up some memories before we start taking Boulder for granted."

"We'll never take Boulder for granted," said Tom, kissing her.

Behind them, they could hear the Zip Code Man in the middle of his act asking for someone to call out their zip code.

"80305," whispered Jill, taking Tom's hand and leading him home.

Open house

Blade met Rickie on the jailbait benches across from the Courthouse. She was young and reckless. He was more than a little reckless himself. Blade stole a car and they drove around for a while. Rickie rifled the glove compartment, but found nothing beyond the owner's manual and registration.

"Let's drive it to the owners' house and leave it in the garage," she said. "They'll go insane trying to figure it out."

"You're insane," laughed Blade. "Where do they live?"

They lived in Rock Creek. It took Blade a while to navigate the pastel clapboard canyons before he found the right house.

"Looks like no one's home," said Blade as they stepped inside. "Probably walking in circles looking for their car."

"Then we better hurry," she said, pulling him upstairs and into the master bedroom.

She was tattooed in the usual places and pierced in some not-so-usual ones. The only marks on him were a few scars from the knife fights that had given him his name. Staring up at the vaulted ceiling, Rickie shivered.

"What's the matter?" he asked.

"I've spent my whole life running away from places like this."

"Relax. We're only here long enough to mess up the sheets and raid the liquor cabinet."

Her voice brightened. "Liquor cabinet?"

Before long they were very pleasantly buzzed on Pepsi and

40-year-old scotch. One thing led to another and Blade carried Rickie back upstairs.

The morning sun woke them, streaming in through a skylight. They stared at each other in horror, listening for the sound of doors opening, footsteps on the stairs, sirens approaching. The house was silent.

They jumped out of bed and began pulling on their clothes. Blade's jeans caught on his foot. He tugged. They tore. He yanked open the nearest drawer and found a pair of khakis, which more or less fit. He yanked open another drawer and found a polo shirt. Seeing him, Rickie opened a closet and found herself a sundress and some sandals.

"Should we take the car?"

"Too risky. We'll walk down a block or so and steal another one."

They had barely walked a block when Blade stopped dead. "Shit," he said. "I left my wallet in my jeans. With all my ID."

They turned around and hurried back. By now the houses around them were coming to life. Blade and Rickie picked up the pace and tried not to catch anyone's eye.

"Is this it?"

"I can't tell."

"Was it pink? This one's pink."

He grabbed her arm and led her across the lawn. Just before they got to the door, a voice called from the next driveway over.

"Hey!" They froze. "I think this is yours." A man in a terry robe tossed Blade a green-bagged newspaper.

"Thanks." Blade kept his head turned, so the guy couldn't get a good look at his face.

Inside, they collapsed against the door. "What were we thinking?" said Blade. "We probably left fingerprints all over the place."

They were giving the surfaces a thorough going-over when the doorbell rang. They looked at each other. It rang again.

They didn't move. There was a knock and the door inched open.

"Anybody home?" It was a delivery guy in a blue uniform. "I need a signature."

Blade kept his head turned as he made a nonsense scribble on the guy's clipboard.

"Have a good one!"

Rickie took the package from Blade, wiped it down and dropped it on the counter. She picked up a shopping bag containing their old clothes and followed him to the door.

Across the street a woman was gardening. Blade pulled Rickie back inside before the woman could look up and see them. They spent the next couple of hours peering through the curtains. Every time they looked, there was someone new outside: kids waiting for the bus, a mailman leisurely feeding mailboxes, women running errands in their SUVs.

Soon it was noon, so Rickie made tuna sandwiches. They each had a beer, then two, then they were into the scotch again.

It was after midnight when Blade awoke in a sweat. He shook Rickie's shoulder. She mumbled "leave me alone" and shrugged his hand away. He thought about sneaking off without her, but he was tired and the bed really was nice. Way nicer than anything he'd slept on in years.

No, his mind screamed. *Get out now while you can!*

He let his eyes close for a half-second, visualizing his escape. Before his next breath he was lost again in sleep, dreaming he was lying next to a girl he barely knew, in a house he didn't recognize, needing desperately to get away before they found him out and everything came crashing down.

Gaia

strid's first glimpse of Gaia was a brown and white blur in the back of a pickup truck that almost ran her bike off Eldorado Springs Road. She shook her fist in rage.

Up the road, around a bend, she heard brakes squeal. A door squeaked opened and shortly after slammed shut. An engine accelerated away. Astrid pedaled hard, rounding the bend. In the tall grass she spied a flash of brown and white.

She dropped her bike and waded into the grass to find an emaciated border collie, lying in a heap. Astrid dropped to her knees and cradled the shivering bundle.

"There now," she whispered. "It's all right. Don't you worry. Astrid's here."

She spent the next six weeks nursing the foundling back to health. Not for the first time, she felt ashamed of her own cruel and heartless species. Gaia licked Astrid's hand. With the light that shone from her liquid brown eyes, she spoke to Astrid for the first time.

"I forgive you," Astrid heard in her mind. She lay her head against Gaia's side and wept for all the pain in the world.

The two were soon inseparable. Gaia followed Astrid from room to room. "Some people might think you're being needy," said Astrid, "but I know you're

only watching over me." Gaia smiled and lay her head
down on her paws.

Gaia revealed her name to Astrid in a dream. Astrid
saw an intense glowing sphere she knew to be the spirit of a Goddess. At first she thought it might be Lilith,
then she realized it was Gaia, the Earth herself, Mother
of us all.

As much as it hurt Astrid to see Gaia's scars, she
came to understand they had shaped Gaia's spirit. Her
suffering had given her the gift of compassion for all living things. And Astrid honored this. She spent extra on
vegetarian dog food. She left the curtains open so Gaia
could watch the squirrels at play. She groomed Gaia by
hand, returning any ticks to the wild.

That Spring the miller moths filled Astrid's condo.
She spent hours catching each one gently in her hands
and taking it out onto the balcony to release.

"You are returning tiny pieces of God's soul to their
proper place," said Gaia.

There was a story in the next morning's Camera
about the Earth Liberation Front. Not for the first time,
Astrid wished she had the courage to join them in their
cause. But Gaia, wiser than she, told Astrid that she had
her own special mission of service to all the innocent
creatures who had no one else.

Hiking on Shanahan Ridge, Astrid and Gaia came
upon a dead skunk. They stopped and said a blessing
for its departed spirit. A little further on, Astrid twisted
her ankle. She tried to walk, but the pain was too
intense. Gaia licked her face until a couple of runners
came along. Between them they carried Astrid down to
their car, and then to the emergency room, Gaia beside
her the whole way.

The doctor told Astrid she would need crutches until
the ankle had completely healed. It tormented Astrid to

see Gaia cooped up all day, so as soon as she could hobble on her crutches, she reached for the leash.

"I'm sorry," she said to Gaia. "You'll have to stay on the leash." Not for the first time, Astrid fumed at her fellow Boulder humans. As if calling themselves "guardians" instead of "owners" were the height of spiritual evolution.

O, the arrogance!

Astrid led Gaia across the parking lot of their condo complex and onto the adjacent sidewalk, hobbling as fast as she could, trying not to hold Gaia back. A voice called from behind.

"On your left!"

Astrid jumped. Gaia cringed. A bicyclist sped past at a recklessly indecent speed. Astrid shook her fist at his back. A little further along they came to a prairie dog colony.

"Look, Gaia!" she called out. "There are babies!"

She spied a small brown shape on the sidewalk. It was a young prairie dog, twitching. She realized it had just been hit by the bicyclist. Gaia spied the hurt animal, too, and bent down to lift it gently in her mouth.

When Astrid reached for the prairie dog she heard a sound she didn't immediately recognize. It was a low, deep growl. And it was coming from Gaia.

"Give it here, Gaia," Astrid said. "That's a good girl."

Gaia opened her jaws and lunged for Astrid's hand, drawing blood. Astrid drew back, staring in horror as Gaia proceeded to kill and eat the tender, young prairie dog.

"Yum," said Gaia.

Code Monkey

Tom's official title was Code Monkey. It said so on the "Our Gang" page of the company website. Milo, the owner, had decided everyone needed cute job titles. Tom suggested "Web Programming Guy."

"Not cute enough," said Milo. "You'll be our Code Monkey." He even had one of the designers paste Tom's head onto a chimp's body for his online photo.

Milo started the company in the late '90s, hoping to jump on the dot-com bandwagon. His vision was a cutting-edge agency with hip clients. Instead the business scraped along building vanilla sites for such paragons of hipness as "Boulder Valley Plumbing Supplies."

Milo's title was "Chief High Mucky-Muck," but his real job was salesman. He spent his days schmoozing on the phone, promising clients impossible things and counting on Tom to save his ass.

The office was a small room above a storefront on the Pearl Street Mall. There were no dividers, no cubicles and no privacy. Everyone sat crammed in front of their machines, like high-tech seamstresses in a 21st-century sweatshop.

At 31, Tom was the old man of the office, not counting the 40-something Milo. The designers were all in their early 20s. They called each other "dude," sported backwards baseball caps and played war games on the office network after hours. Every day at 5:00, one of them would shout, "It's Quake o'clock, dudes!" Within seconds, Tom would be bombarded by the splats, thuds and screams of digitized mayhem. He would sigh, hunch over his keyboard and get back to saving Milo's ass.

Every so often one of the dudes would invite Tom to join in. "Come on, dude. Shed some mutant blood. It'll keep you sane."

Tom would politely decline. Out of the corner of his eye he'd see the others make faces behind his back. Let them. Someone had to be the adult.

Tom's breaking point came late one Friday as he was laboring to finish up some JavaScript. A hand appeared on his shoulder. He looked up. It was Milo.

"Tom, buddy, I hope you don't have any plans for the weekend…"

Tom's stomach churned. He'd been looking forward to painting the garage. And Jill had made him promise to go to a matinee on Sunday. He shrugged his shoulders. Milo clapped him on the back.

"Good man. I promised Gladys we'd add a shopping cart to her site by Monday. You can whip one up, right?"

Milo headed off to make the weekly bank run. Tom stared at his monitor, his outside calm, but his insides churning. With a click of his mouse, he opened PhotoShop, a program he didn't know very well. He was a programmer, not a designer. But he had a certain basic competence.

First he imported a clip-art pig. Next he copied Milo's photo from the "Our Gang" web page and pasted the head onto the pig's body. Underneath, in big letters, he put Milo's title, changing the "M"s to "F"s.

Tom stared at his handiwork, feeling a sense of emotional release. For a moment, he longed for the guts to post it live on the website.

"Dudes," said a voice behind Tom. "Check it out!"

Tom reached to delete the file, but a hand reached over his shoulder and grabbed his mouse.

"Nice start, dude, but you need to crop the head more." The dude shoved Tom out of the way and went to work. The other dudes gathered around and offered advice.

"Throw a drop shadow under the body."

"Add some horns and a pitchfork."

Tom tried to retake his seat, but they ignored him. Suddenly the big color printer whirred to life and a printout slid out. Tom stared at it in horror. It contained his original graphic now retouched into a work of malicious comic art. At the bottom was a note: "Give our Code Monkey the weekend off or we all quit." One by one, each dude signed it. Tom was speechless, fighting the tears which welled up in his eyes.

"What the hell is this?" a voice boomed behind Tom. He turned to see Milo staring at the printout. No one said anything for a long moment. Then Milo burst into laughter. "Hey, Tom, the next time you want a weekend off, just ask." He clapped Tom on the shoulder. "What the hey, Gladys can just wait on that shopping cart."

"Dudes," someone shouted. "It's half past Quake o'clock!"

Everyone stayed after, Tom included. He even let himself to be talked into playing. As a total newbie, he was killed 23 times. But he had never felt so alive.

Home cooking

Dickie Sr. waited until just before bedtime to break the news to Tish. "You know that hedge fund my brother Greg was raving about?"

"The one I said we should stay away from?" She stared into the mirror, brushing her hair.

"Yes, well, I thought it would be fun to dabble a bit."

She closed her eyes. "How much did you lose?"

It was a long moment before he answered. "Everything."

The next morning at breakfast they called a family meeting. Dickie Jr. and Alicia were annoyed at having their schedules interrupted until they realized the seriousness of the problem.

"Does this mean I can't go to Cancun on Spring Break?"

"I'm still getting a 4x4 for graduation, right?"

"Forget Cancun," said Tish. "Forget the 4x4. Forget staying here in Devil's Thumb. This time your father has screwed up so badly we'll be lucky to afford Gunbarrel."

They were all silent.

"Can you get a job?" Dickie Jr. said finally.

"I inherited everything," said Dickie Sr. "I have absolutely no salable skills."

"This really sucks!" There was a touch of panic in Alicia's voice. "What are we going to do?"

"Maybe we could start a home-based business," said Dickie Sr.

"You and Mom selling Amway?" Dickie Jr. rolled his eyes.

"At least your father's trying to be helpful," said Tish.

"What we need," said Dickie Sr. "is a product we can make at home out of readily available ingredients and sell at a big markup."

Alicia and Dickie Jr. looked at each other and said two words:

"Crystal meth!"

Dickie Jr. went online and found an easy-to-follow recipe which he downloaded and printed out. Tish and Alicia assembled a shopping list.

"Cold medicine, antifreeze, drain cleaner," said Dickie Sr., glancing over the list. "How are we going to afford all this?"

"We can save by buying generic," said Alicia.

"That's my girl," said Tish.

"Wow," said Alicia as she and Tish headed out to shop. "You and Daddy never trusted us to help with anything important before. It feels kind of good."

While the ladies were gone the two Dickies prepared the downstairs. They moved out the pool table and cleared off the wet bar. They set up the camping stove and brought down glassware — the good crystal, of course.

"Hey, that's almost poetic," said Dickie Jr.

When Tish and Alicia returned, the guys helped unload the Range Rover and everyone trooped downstairs to cook up the first batch. Spirits were high and things went off without a hitch. Thinking about it later, Tish realized it had been the first day the four of them had successfully spent together without a therapist present.

Two days later Dickie Sr. and Dickie Jr. put on matching leather jackets and climbed into Dickie Sr.'s Boxter. They cruised down the Turnpike and south on Sheridan Avenue.

"There's a Harley," said Dickie Jr.

They pulled into the parking lot of a dingy bar just as a burly guy came out and headed for the bike.

"Free sample?" Dickie Sr. called to him.

Three days later they returned. The burly guy was nowhere

to be seen, but there were two bikers waiting in his place.

"Where's your friend?" asked Dickie Sr.

"Psych ward," said one of the bikers. "Hasn't slept for three days."

"We'll take every ounce you can give us," said the other biker.

Alicia kept the records. Dickie Jr. oversaw production. Dickie Sr. handled distribution. In three months they were out of debt. In six, they had racked up a healthy profit. Tish invested it in blue chips, setting up the account so Dickie Sr. couldn't make withdrawals without her signature.

The kids' grades improved dramatically. Especially Alicia's math, which had always been her weakness. Dickie Jr.'s chemistry teacher made special note of his impeccable lab technique. Dickie Sr. and Tish were so busy they had no time for outside lovers and found themselves forced to rekindle their sex life. With a gang of murderous and unforgiving bikers counting on regular delivery of product, the family quickly learned to work together. Old areas of conflict seemed somehow trivial. They soon terminated with their family therapist who remarked on their vastly improved communication.

There were elections in the fall, and Dickie Sr. talked the family into making a big donation to the tough-on-drugs Republican candidate for DA.

"It's the right thing to do," he said. "And it'll help keep prices up."

At Christmas, the family gathered in the den to share their new-found closeness and toast their great good fortune.

"To us," said Dickie.

"To us."

They all drank deeply, savoring the moment. Other than a sharp increase in overdoses and drug-related homicides statewide, it had been a good year for everyone.

Rave on

S kyler was feeding a Red Bull through the self-scan at King Soopers when The Idea hit him. "Please place the item in the bag." It arrived in his brain fully formed and complete, demanding to be brought to life.

"Please place the item in the bag."

He was frozen in place by the transcendent audacity it represented.

"Please place the item in the bag."

Nothing in his 22 years of life had prepared him for something so subversively delicious, so sublimely outrageous, so —

"Place the item in the freaking bag, dude!" said a voice from behind him.

"Sorry." He placed the Red Bull in the bag, slid a five into the bill acceptor, took his change and receipt, and hurried off to tell his housemates.

"Spaces Sit Empty and Tax Revenues Plunge!" screamed the day's headlines. "Will the Business Community Do Something?"

Abby and Savannah were napping when Skyler burst in and dropped onto the waterbed. By the time the waves died down to ripples, The Idea had crossed from his brain to theirs. All three sat frozen, their minds' eyes wide, their synapses popping like illegal fireworks.

"We have to do it," said Abby finally.

"We have to do it this Saturday," said Savannah.

Abby took charge of arranging the talent. Skyler went to

work securing equipment and materials. Savannah had an idea about getting access. "That guy Steve I hooked up with last week at the Fox is a security guard," she said.

"Can we trust him?" said Skyler.

"He hates his job, worships my bod and has a complete set of keys."

"Sweet," said Abby.

That night back in the waterbed they shared a carton of Phish Food and updated each other on their individual progress. With each success story the collected energy gathered intensity. Before long Abby licked some caramel off Skyler's chin. Savannah nuzzled Abby's neck. No one got much sleep that night.

"Boulder's Pain is Broomfield's Gain!" thundered the next day's front page. "Will the City Council Do Something?"

They put the word out on a strictly viral basis. Direct transmission only with maximum precautions to prevent accidental release. The Idea spread through the city in a delicate web of contact "hi's."

Steve came over in the afternoon with a set of smuggled blueprints. They spread them on the kitchen table and finalized The Plan. When everyone at last agreed it was flawless, Abby brought out the Phish Food, and Steve joined them on the waterbed.

No one got any sleep that night.

"Broomfield's Gain is Boulder's Shame!" raged the editorial page. "Who Will Do Something?"

The Day dawned early and clear. Under Steve's watchful if slightly bleary eye, a truck backed up to the dock and many hands made short work of off-loading. Inside, one team cleared away the scattered rubble, while another set up systems for the delivery of visual and auditory overstimulation.

Skyler checked off each item on his clipboard. Just before dusk the regular staff of security guards rotated off. They were replaced by Steve and a few trusted allies.

As the first stars were appearing in the sky, the people began to arrive. One by one they made their way inside the empty temple of business to wait in silence. When the last clerk shuttered the last storefront, Steve made a quick sweep of the building.

"All clear," he reported back.

"Let's do it," said Skyler.

The place exploded with light and sound. A roar went up from the waiting crowd. They began to move as one organism, fueled by youth, hormones and all the pent-up energy in the world. Hour after hour they gave themselves over to joy and motion. A mass of revelers filling the abandoned cathedral of commerce to partake in ecstatic communion.

Up and down the frozen escalators the music rang, penetrating every nook and echoing off the empty make-up counters and underwear racks.

Just before midnight, Steve got a squawk on the hand-held radio. "Supervisor at 12 o'clock!"

Steve gave Skyler a frantic sign. Skyler pulled the master switch, cutting all power and plunging the room into darkness. As if in a trance, the dancers ignored the silence, continuing to move, swaying, pulsing, following an inner groove in the absolute darkness.

The supervisor entered the building for an unscheduled security check. He strolled the empty arcades, his footsteps echoing in the gloom. If any trace came to his ears of a thousand breaths flowing together or 2,000 feet moving in unison, it seemed only the ghost of his own youth.

Skyler, Abby and Savannah found each other across the crowded floor and wrapped their arms around each other's sweat-drenched bodies.

"One Generation's Trash is Another's Treasure!" they whispered to themselves. "We Did Something!"

Eggs

Jill was beyond exhausted. She was nearing the end of a truly crazy shift. One gunshot, two coronaries, and innumerable cuts, sprains, fractures and asthma attacks. Not to mention the looney tune with the twisted ankle who went into hysterics when Jill wouldn't let her mutt into the examining room.

"Sorry," Jill explained. "Only guide animals are allowed."

"But she is a guide animal," insisted the woman. "She's my spirit guide."

Boulder. You gotta love it.

Instead of heading straight home to sleep, Jill made her way through the hospital from the ER to the big glass window. She stood and looked in at the tiny sleeping faces.

Her eggs smiled.

The neonatal nurse on duty was Carol, a friend of Jill's. She waved Jill in. Jill cradled a tiny newborn in her arms and crooned softly. The tiny eyes opened for a second, then closed again.

Her eggs sang.

"You've got it bad, girl," said Carol. "It's time you had a little one of your own."

"Tell me about it," said Jill. "Or better yet, tell my pig-headed husband."

Jill had expected the move to Boulder to lead naturally to starting a family. But all the new home rep-

31

resented to Tom was a big mortgage payment.

"We need to build our savings back up before we take on any more responsibilities," he'd said in his most reasonable tone of voice.

It made her want to scream.

Jill handed the sleeping infant to Carol and went out to catch her bus home.

The Skip driver was young and cute. He smiled at Jill, his eyes quickly appraising her and signaling their approval. She smiled back, doing a little appraising of her own.

Her eggs said, "Jump him!"

She took her seat instead. The irony was Jill hadn't grown up dreaming of motherhood. No dolls or babysitting for her. After adolescence she'd been an unabashed party girl, choosing her men on the basis of looks, dance moves and ability to match her drink for drink.

Then her eggs woke up.

All at once men were potential fathers. Party boys lost all ability to fascinate. Suddenly, steady earners and serious planners made her motor run. And Tom was the most serious planner she'd ever met in her life.

The bus reached Baseline, and Jill got out. She crossed the Base-Mar parking lot and continued on past the closed Italian restaurant. She passed a man pushing a double stroller. The twins inside stared up at her, their little mouths hanging open. She cooed at them. The man smiled and gave her a wink.

"Grab him!" shouted her eggs.

How could things have gotten so screwed up so fast? Why should she, a grown woman, have to beg a man, her husband, for the privilege of fulfilling her natural destiny? She was 29 years old, for God's sake. Her eggs were 20 percent less fertile than they were two years ago! She wanted to scream, "Make me pregnant NOW or get out of my way!"

If Tom could spend just one shift in the ER with her. Let him see people whose had their lives all nice and tidy until the day their car got broadsided or the tumor appeared. Let him grasp just how little the universe cares about our illusions of "security."

When her pills ran out last month, she hadn't bothered refilling the prescription. She'd be damned if she was going to drug her body to prevent the one thing she wanted most in life. If Tom wanted to postpone their family, let him use the birth control.

Actually, at the present, the point was moot. For the last three weeks she and Tom hadn't even touched each other. It was like once they'd fulfilled their dream of moving to Boulder, their closeness had vanished. They were no longer on the same page.

Jill finally got home a little before 7 a.m. She was sticky, so she decided to shower before crawling into bed. She was rinsing off when the shower curtain opened and Tom stepped under the spray with her.

"Hey there," he said, his voice warmer than it had been in weeks. "How was your shift?"

"Crazy," she said, knowing that this was the worst possible time to bring up the baby issue, but knowing she had to anyway. Before she could, he took her face in his hands and kissed her. She melted into the kiss. He reached around her, not breaking the kiss, and turned off the water.

Tom pulled Jill out of the tub, across the bathroom and into the bedroom. As she fell into the cool sheets with him, she knew she should tell him she was off the pill.

"Tell him tomorrow," said her eggs.

Gay lettuce

Are you insane?" said Todd's friends when he announced he was moving to Colorado. "Do you want to end up on a barbwire fence in a made-for-TV movie?"

"Boulder's supposedly very gay-friendly," he said. "Besides, if I want to go to Naropa I don't have a choice." So he packed up his espresso machine and his Gershwin CDs and made his way west.

He thought he'd prepared himself for the culture shock, but he was wrong.

"It may be gay-friendly, but there's not a drop of gay energy here," he complained on the phone to his best friend, Ray. "I walk down the street and no one even meets my eyes. I've never felt so invisible."

"So give up this craziness," said Ray, "and come home."

Instead Todd went to a gay support group he found through a flyer on the Naropa bulletin board. Everyone was warm and welcoming, but he couldn't believe the level of the discussion. Again and again the participants spoke of "coming to terms with my gayness." He felt like he was 15 and back in Iowa. As soon as he could, Todd slipped out the back.

"Hey!"

Todd turned around to find a young man in Italian jeans and black Kenneth Cole Romas. "Are you really so superior to the rest of us?" said the young man. "Or are you just arrogant?"

Todd surprised himself by saying, "Why don't you come have coffee with me and find out?"

Todd and the young man, who introduced himself as Mark, walked the Mall to Starbucks. Along the way, Todd noticed Mark checking him out. He suddenly wished he'd paid more attention to his outfit that day — baggy jeans and that stupid Tinky Winky T-shirt he'd had for ages.

"What exactly drove you away tonight?" said Mark, settling into an armchair with a skinny double latte, "Coming out stories bore you?"

"Not at all," said Todd, blowing on his white chocolate mocha. "But what counts is what you do after you come out."

"And what did you do?"

"I moved to Chicago along with every other gay Midwestern boy with any sense." Todd sipped his mocha. "I mean, for God's sake, why settle for being an outsider when you can live where everybody gets you? Where you never have to hide? Where you can flaunt your outrageous self in the street? Hold hands on the sidewalk? Kiss under a street lamp?"

"You must miss it," said Mark.

"We have an expression back home," said Todd. "'Gay lettuce.' It means even if you want something as simple as a head of lettuce, you know you can find it at a gay grocer. Whatever you need is right there in your neighborhood." His voice caught in his throat. "I miss gay lettuce."

They talked until Starbucks closed, then Todd gave Mark his Hotmail address but not his phone number. There was some chemistry, yes, and the beginnings of a connection, but the last thing he needed right now was another doomed affair.

"Let me get this straight," said Ray after Todd called to tell him everything. "You meet this cute guy who you really connect with and who wants to see you again. You're right. It's hopeless."

"We come from completely different cultures," said Todd. "There's no way it can work."

Over the next week, Mark and Todd exchanged a series of long e-mails in which they discovered their mothers both had the same middle name, they'd each owned a rat terrier as a boy, and their fathers had both died young. With each e-mail, they went a little deeper until Todd realized he was sharing things he had never told another soul in his life. Finally he broke down and gave Mark his phone number.

"Okay," he said when Mark called him, "here's the bottom line. I had it all in Chicago — except a healthy relationship. Every man I dated turned out to be emotionally unavailable. So, if you're going to disappear when things get real, please tell me now."

"This feels pretty real already," said Mark. "And I'm still here. So, can I see you again?"

From the moment he said yes, Todd was an emotional wreck. He couldn't sleep. He couldn't eat. He couldn't do anything but obsessively clean his apartment and agonize over what to wear. He was changing his shirt for the third time when the doorbell rang. When he opened the door, his eyes met Mark's and a current of electricity went through him. He knew he was in trouble deep.

Mark handed him a wrapped bouquet. "Welcome to Boulder," he said.

Wordlessly, Todd undid the paper to find an absolutely gorgeous head of red leaf lettuce.

Crystal blue

Before Crystal even opened her eyes she knew something was very wrong. She couldn't say how she knew. She just did. She sent her consciousness into different points in her physical body but couldn't detect any problems. She moved on to her emotional body and then her spiritual body. Nothing and nothing. She sat up slowly and reached for the phone.

"Lissa," she said, "something's wrong, but I don't know what."

"I'll meet you at Vitamin Cottage."

Crystal folded her futon, threw on a wrap skirt over her yoga-tard and collected her supplements. Lissa was talking with a cute young clerk in the Antioxidants section when Crystal walked in.

"Doug wants to know if you're taking any phyto-nutrients," said Lissa.

"Lycopene, 15 milligrams, three times a day," said Crystal, handing the clerk a bag with all her supplements. He looked through them, nodding appreciatively.

"Awesome," he said. "You're doing everything possible for a woman your age."

Ouch.

They walked over to Whole Foods and ordered Jamba Powerboosts, taking them out to the sidewalk tables in front of the store.

"Could it be some leftover energy from the Holotropic Breathwork workshop last weekend?" asked Lissa.

"No," said Crystal. "I released on such a deep level that I slept for 14 hours Sunday night."

"Has anyone new come into your life?"

"Well, Amy wasn't available for my shiatsu session yesterday, so I had to settle for Sasha."

"There you go."

"But Sasha's worked on me two or three times before and I've never felt anything like this."

They dumped their empty cups in the trash and drove to yoga. In the middle of class, from the Downward-Facing Dog position, Lissa whispered, "Could it be sexual tension?"

Crystal shook her head. "Alex and I have an arrangement. Strictly tantric."

Lissa had a lunch appointment she couldn't break, so Crystal called Rachel, her astrologer, and talked her into an emergency appointment.

"Well," said Rachel, consulting Crystal's chart, "I don't see any major disturbances at this time. Unless this could be due to the Capricorn influence I've been warning you about."

"No, I figured out that was Tony, my ex's lawyer. He hit on me after the final mediation session. I remembered your warning and only went out with him a couple of times before I broke it off."

Crystal took herself home to her studio apartment and closed all the blinds. She lit every candle she owned and saged the room completely. Then she undressed and positioned her zabuton cushion in the exact middle of the room. She sat in a half lotus and took a dozen yoga breaths. Using everything she had learned from the many classes she had taken over her life, she purified herself. She released ego, then conscious mind, then desire, then attachment, cleansing layer by layer so that any impurity would reveal itself.

But nothing appeared.

When she brought herself back to consciousness, it was already dark outside. Crystal sat in the candle-flicker, panic rising in her body. This wasn't like her. She had always had a natural gift, according to every teacher in every class. She'd been the one to go deepest, the one with the surest intuition, the one most capable of insight and understanding. Why had her gift now abandoned her when she needed it most?

She broke down and took a couple of Xanax from the secret little bottle in the very back of her closet. The familiar fog was coming in on little cat feet when Lissa arrived with organic salads and a bottle of wine.

"Any luck?" she asked, pouring the wine.

"No," said Crystal. "What is wrong with me?"

"Don't worry," said Lissa, "The answer will come as soon as you stop looking."

After Lissa left, Crystal made herself some Sleepy Time tea, swallowed a couple of melatonins, unrolled her futon and crawled under the comforter. She read the daily affirmation from her dog-eared copy of Women Who Do Too Much. Then she blew out the last candle.

Just before she slipped off to sleep, a strange moment of clarity came over her. It was as if she were above herself, looking down. She saw a 42-year-old woman with no career, no family and no community — not counting people she wrote checks to. A woman who flitted from one path to another, like a butterfly in a wind tunnel. A woman so busy reaching, she never touched — and was never touched herself. A woman who would some day be mourned but who would never be missed.

Just as quickly as it had come, the moment passed and she was asleep. A dreamless sleep from which she would awaken the next morning, pure and refreshed and remembering nothing — ready for another day in the center of her own special universe.

Silent treatment

Tom couldn't put his finger on what was bothering him. He'd been working for over an hour beside Jill. It was early Saturday morning, and they were scraping the house to get it ready for painting. The morning air was cool with a crisp scent of evergreen. The world seemed to be waking up slowly around them as they worked quietly side by side.

Quietly.

That was it.

Jill had been with him for over an hour and she hadn't said a word. That wasn't like her, to put it mildly. Tom looked over at her. She was diligently using the wire brush to loosen flakes of old paint, just like he'd shown her. Her attention was focused on her work. She didn't seem upset. He couldn't recall anything he'd done to earn him the silent treatment. Besides, that wasn't Jill's style. If she was upset over something, he would hear about it. In fact, pretty much anything she thought or felt, he heard about.

That's why it was spooky that she was so...quiet. He glanced over at her again. She was scraping away with the wire brush.

"Nice morning," he ventured. "Cool and crisp."

She just nodded.

Very spooky.

They broke for lunch a little before noon. Tom, to score a few brownie points just in case, comman-

deered the kitchen and made Boca burgers. They ate on
the back porch. Jill brought out a paperback and kept
her nose buried in it the entire time. Was this some
kind of turnabout-is-fair-play scheme to pay him back
for the times he'd read at the table? If so, it was back-
firing. Tom found himself relishing the quiet.

After lunch Tom suggested a ride. They climbed on
their bikes and rode the two blocks to the trail. On the
way they passed the ice cream truck with its warbly
melody that was a strange blend of an old hymn and
"Look for the Union Label."

They headed east under the Turnpike. At Williams
Village Tom picked up the pace, taking it beyond Jill's
usual comfort zone. He waited for her to holler for him
to slow down. Instead, when he hazarded a glance over
his shoulder, she was right in his slipstream, matching
him pedal for pedal.

That night they ate at Japango, out back on the
enclosed patio. Tom ordered a flask of pearl saki. He
started to pour some for Jill, but she held up a hand to
block him and reached for her water instead.

"What a night, huh?" said Tom, tossing back a cup
of saki. "Say, did you notice that scratch on the bumper
of the Corolla? I'm going to have to hit it with some
touch-up paint. And what about that ice cream truck
song? Like some weird blend of that old hymn and
'Look for the Union Label.'"

Listen to him prattle on. Could this be her point?
Was she trying to show him that he'd been leaving it to
her to do all the conversational heavy lifting in the marriage? Well, enough of that. He was the introvert in the
relationship. He could damn well tolerate a little silence
over dinner. He smiled at Jill and fortified himself with
another cup of saki.

Their orders arrived and Tom and Jill picked away

at their Boulder bowls in silence. Tom glanced at the other tables on the patio. Every one seemed to be filled with couples enjoying animated conversations. He and Jill were the only ones not talking. How must they look sitting there stone faced over their food? Like a couple with nothing to say to each other. A marriage in trouble. A relationship on the brink.

He racked his brain for something to say. He'd used up all his small talk earlier in the day. All that was left to say was what was really on his mind. And that was dangerous. Wait a minute. What was the matter with him? Why was he sitting here scared of his own wife, for heaven's sake? Was he a husband or a mouse?

"We can't keep putting off the issue of rebuilding our savings," he started, sipping some more saki. "We need to commit to a dollar amount to put away each month."

Tom waited for the inevitable blast from Jill. She hated talking money. Especially in public. The last time he'd tried, she'd made a scene right there at the table. But her eyes stayed on her food. So he plunged on.

"What if we started with $500? I admit it's aggressive. It would mean me finding some outside projects and you taking extra shifts. And, of course, we'd have to postpone starting a family." He held his breath. "What do you think?"

Jill glanced up from her Boulder bowl.

"I'm pregnant," she said.

Sacred gas

Kyle was walking after midnight when he heard the gentle cry. He froze on the sidewalk. Yes, there it was. A soft but steady keening, otherworldly and impossibly sad. He stood for what may have been hours, bearing silent witness to the wordless song of grief.

The next morning he found his way to the same spot. He couldn't hear anything for all the traffic noise, air conditioners and music from passing cars. But he was patient and eventually his ears caught the unmistakable note of quiet agony. It seemed to be coming from a white plastic pipe on the roof of a small house. Kyle looked and looked, but he could find no reason for the house or the pipe to be so sad.

A woman eventually stepped out the door.

"Excuse me," said Kyle, in his gentlest voice. "What's the purpose of the pipe on your roof?"

"That?" she said, following his finger. "I think it's part of the radon thingy in the basement."

Kyle thanked her and took himself to the library. He hopped on a public computer and Googled his way to the EPA website where he was informed that radon was a "gaseous radioactive element." The site went on to claim that radon seeped into houses and gave people lung cancer. This disturbed Kyle. He couldn't reconcile these so-called "facts" with the unmistakable emotion he'd heard with his own ears.

He walked to Kinko's and put together a simple flier which he took all around Boulder. He put them up in health food stores, alternative medical offices, organic restaurants, coffee shops and every other location he could talk his way into.

The first meeting of the "Study Group to Investigate the Existence of Underground Angels" convened the following Friday evening in a study room of the library. Eight people showed up, including a librarian who complained that Kyle hadn't officially reserved the space. Kyle apologized with his most sincere smile, and soon the meeting was in full swing. Kyle soon had the group spellbound with his passionate tale of an immense governmental cover-up.

"What if the substance the EPA calls 'radon' is, in fact, the energetic bodies of Earth-bound angels?" he said. "And what if the very point of their existence is to enter our bodies through our breath and make us holy?"

At this point, half the group walked out. The other half, including the librarian, stayed for another hour before following Kyle on an impromptu field trip to the little house. They stood in an awkward cluster, each nodding to indicate they'd heard. At the same time, none of them seemed all that convinced the sound was anything more than air rushing through a pipe. Before they could voice their doubts, Kyle boosted himself up onto the roof of the house. He made his way over to the pipe, lowered his face to the opening and sucked in a lungful.

Suddenly, he jumped to his feet, bounded across the roof and leapt to the ground in front of the startled group. His eyes aglow, Kyle strode away down the sidewalk, the others following at his heels.

Over the next few weeks, the young group grew rapidly. As each member felt ready, he or she would re-enact Kyle's nocturnal rooftop inhalation. (When the first two initiates each broke a leg leaping from the roof, the ceremony was modified to allow for the use of a ladder.) As might be expected, the residents of the house at first objected to total strangers tromping over their roof, but after a few minutes with Kyle at his persuasive best, they were climbing the roof to breathe in angels of their own.

Kyle's contagious passion fueled the burgeoning movement. Meanwhile, a core of volunteers formed to take over the practical side of things. They organized meetings, filed for tax-exempt status as a religious organization and began petitioning the EPA to overturn its bigoted position on radon.

As for Kyle, he began dropping out of sight every so often. When located, he would be almost comatose with grief for all the angels perishing with no human hosts to breathe them in. The group comforted him as best they could and redoubled their efforts to recruit new members.

Exactly two months after Kyle's original inspiration, he was again standing in front of the little house after midnight. This time, however, he was discovered by a pair of Boulder police officers who recognized him from previous encounters. They delivered him to the Emergency Room, where he was also well known. He was administered his usual dose of lithium to stabilize his bipolar symptoms and an anti-psychotic to return him more or less to reality.

No such remedy was available for the rest of the group.

High school heat

Darren pulled into the faculty lot on the first day of the new school year. He grabbed his satchel, checked to make sure he had his keys, and locked the Taurus GL. On his way inside, he took a moment to pat the firm bulge under his left armpit.

"What're you carrying?" asked Alex from the History department, coming up beside him.

"Glock 30," answered Darren.

Alex whistled. "That's some righteous hardware. I favor the H and K myself. Ten-round magazine. .45ACP. What's your load?"

"230 grain hydra-shocks. Guaranteed to stop a rampaging elephant. Or at least a sophomore. Right, son?" Darren asked a passing student. When the boy didn't answer, Darren dropped his satchel and drew the Glock in one easy, practiced motion. "I said — *right, son?*"

The boy froze. "Sir, yes, sir."

Darren eyed the panicked student over his weapon for a long, tense moment before relaxing and holstering his piece. "Run along," he said, tousling the boy's hair. "Wouldn't want to be late to class now, would you?"

"Sir, no, sir." The boy ran off down the hall.

In the classroom, Darren set aside his standard welcome speech in favor of an impromptu civics lesson. "As you are all no doubt aware, one month ago the state legislature, with the enthusiastic support of the Bush Administration and the Ashcroft Justice Department, enacted the Colorado School

Safety Initiative. This landmark legislation grants automatic concealed carry permits to all public school teachers."

Darren took a moment to smile and study the class. They were, to a student, sitting upright in their desks. They also seemed better dressed than in years past. And, unless he was imagining it, there was a new look of respect, and yes, fear, in their faces — except for one petite blonde in the front row whose eyes glistened with a certain simmering excitement.

"Now, this being Boulder," Darren continued, "many of your parents are no doubt opposed to such a straightforward and common-sense approach to stopping school violence. But I think they will soon see the wisdom — "

Before he could finish his sentence, a loud blast came from somewhere down the hall. The students dove under their desks. Darren rose, Glock drawn, and moved smoothly to the doorway.

"Stay down," he barked over his shoulder. The hall was empty, but not for long. Out of each doorway, in precise unison, stepped an armed teacher. As one, they moved silently toward the direction of the blast. Darren took the lead with Alex bringing up the rear.

"Sounded like it came from the Science department," whispered Myron from Mathematics.

They crept down the empty hallway, weapons drawn and safeties off. Darren glanced back, swelling with pride at the sight of his fellow faculty members following him bravely into danger — even old Miss Abernathy who he remembered from his own days as a student. She caught his look and hefted her Walther P99 with its patented Moroni grip.

"I've been a closet NRA member for decades," she whispered. "Someone's got to stand up for the right of decent people not to live in fear."

They reached the Science department. A thin wisp of smoke filtered out from under the door to the Chemistry lab.

"I'm going in," hissed Darren. "Cover me."

The others split into two groups, pressing themselves against the lockers on either side of the doorway. On Darren's signal, Alex and Myron kicked in the door while Alice, the Social Sciences Chair, laid down a withering burst of cover fire from her TEC-9.

Darren dove low into the lab, rolling sideways and simultaneously shooting out the overhead fluorescents. Screams filled the air from frightened students diving beneath the lab tables.

Darren rolled gracefully to his feet, sweeping the Glock in precise arcs from one corner of the lab to the other. Through the cloud of smoke and cordite, he saw Jillian, the newest member of the Physical Sciences faculty. She smiled sheepishly and held up the shattered remnants of a glass beaker.

"False alarm," she said. "Just a Bunsen burner turned up a little too high."

Darren lowered his weapon as the teachers all shared a moment of relieved laughter.

"Can we come out now?" said one of the huddled students.

"Sure," said Darren, leveling his pistol at the emerging student. "Bang!" The student shrieked, dropping in a dead faint. "But next time remember to say 'sir.'"

"Darren?"

He turned, irritated, looking for the source of the interruption.

"Darren, honey. You're going to be late."

Darren sat up and rubbed the sleep from his eyes. A feeling of profound disappointment descended on him as the last tendrils of the dream evaporated.

Not yet, he thought to himself, *but some day*. This was Colorado after all.

Some day soon.

Pregnant glow

Jill lifted her head, reached for the flush lever, then pulled herself to her feet. She opened the stall door, walked to the sink and rinsed out her mouth. This was the fourth time today. *Morning sickness my ass — more like any-damn-hour-of-the-day-or-night sickness.* She checked her reflection in the mirror, making sure she hadn't spattered her uniform. Three more hours to go on her shift. She didn't know how she was going to make it.

"You Okay?" said Glynnis out in the hallway.

"I'm not sure I remember what OK feels like," said Jill.

"Why don't you go home? I'll cover for you."

"Tom would kill me. He says with the baby coming, we need to work more hours, not less."

"You get your ass on home." Glynnis pushed Jill toward the door. "If he gives you any crap, just slip him some ipecac and see how much work he gets done while hugging the toilet."

On the bus home, Jill slumped in her seat, wrapping her thoughts around her like a musty shawl. She should be happy and excited, but all she felt was dread. This was Boulder, after all, where people biked, ran, climbed, skied, boarded, bladed, kayaked — everything except tying themselves down to a squalling infant. That's what people in Louisville did.

What craziness had driven her to throw her life

50

away? No more spur-of-the-moment trail runs. No more mall crawls. No more spontaneous romantic get-aways. No more romance, period. In fact, Tom was barely speaking to her.

All he'd said when she broke the news to him at the restaurant was, "How did this happen?"

"How the hell do you think it happened?" she'd snapped at him.

What was wrong with her? How had she expected him to react after she ambushed him? And in public, no less. Still, would it have killed him to take her hand and say, "Oh, darling, I'm so ecstatic! A brand new life, equal parts you and me, and it's growing right now inside you!"

It hadn't gone any better when she'd called her mother. "Oh dear," her mother had said. "Are you sure you're ready for this?"

"Can't you just be happy for me, Mother?"

"Of course I'm happy! I only meant are you sure you're ready for the varicose veins, the stretch marks, the hemorrhoids? Not to mention the pain. You know, no one ever really prepares you for how bad it is."

It wasn't just her mother. Every parent Jill met seemed to delight in tormenting her. "Enjoy your free-dom," they'd say. Or, "Get caught up on your sleep. You'll need it."

As for her childless friends, they just looked at her like she was insane. And she was — or at least she had been. A biologically-induced, temporary insanity that had evaporated the exact instant the pink line appeared in the round window of the E.P.T.

Jill glanced out the bus window as a motorcycle went past with a dog riding on the gas tank. The dog had its own little helmet. It looked at Jill, its mouth open in a big sloppy smile, full of the sheer joy of being young and free and alive. Jill burst into tears. A woman across the aisle leaned over and asked her what was wrong.

"I'm pregnant," wailed Jill.

"I hope you're not planning to do something rash," said the woman, pulling a brochure out of her purse. "We have Christian counselors — "

"You don't understand," Jill said between sobs. "I *want* it. Or at least I thought I did when I 'forgot' to tell my husband I'd stopped taking the pill. But now all I feel is depressed and bloated and selfish and I wouldn't blame him if he walked out on me!"

The woman patted Jill's hand uncomfortably, and slid back across the aisle to her own seat.

Jill got out at Baseline and trudged through the Taco Bell parking lot. She passed the closed Italian restaurant which was now opening up as a Mexican restaurant.

It started to rain just as she got to Moorhead. She was soaked by the time she walked up the front walk to the house and stood on the porch. She couldn't bring herself to go inside, paralyzed with fear that when she opened the door, all Tom's stuff would be gone.

She didn't know how long she was standing there before the door opened and Tom stepped out. "Get in here this instant and dry off." He pushed her inside, sat her down, fetched a towel and began drying her off. "You've got to start taking better care of yourself, Jill," he said. "After all, you're carrying our baby."

She closed her eyes, her heart soaring in her chest. It wasn't "Oh, darling, I'm so ecstatic," but it would do.

Lucky

leanor kept her sense of humor through almost all of that terrible year. She brought party hats for Frank's final chemo session and took a picture of him with the oncology nurses. It was on the coffin at the funeral, next to the faded portrait of a young Frank with Eleanor and little Benny.

A few months later Eleanor sold her beloved Chautauqua home to cover Frank's medical bills. She threw a big moving-out party in which she gave her friends back the ugliest gift each had given her and Frank over the years. Many laughs were shared over the tie-dyed place mats, the harvest gold fondue set, the Leroy Neiman print.

Once Eleanor and her beloved Persian Guinevere had settled into their bland new condo, she prepared herself for the next challenge: reestablishing a social life. "I've played more canasta, drank more tea and seen more matinees in the last month than the entire rest of my life," she told Ben at their weekly lunch together.

"You thinking about dating yet, Ma?" he said.

"Are you kidding me? It's a jungle out there. As Myra says, 'If they're younger than you, they're after your purse. If they're older than you, they're after a nurse.'"

The final blow came when Guinevere ran between Eleanor's legs and out under the wheels of a passing car. She rushed her to the animal hospital where the vet, a kindly, heavyset young man, told her there was nothing they could do. So Eleanor stroked Guinevere's head and whispered softly to her as the vet shaved the hair off a forearm, found a vein and slipped the needle in.

Eleanor signed the cremation form, drove herself home and fell to pieces. She didn't know how many days passed with the curtains drawn before Ben was banging at her door. Then he was sitting on the side of her bed, saying "Oh, Ma" and stroking her arm. A part of her mind thought, "Looking for a vein to slip the needle in?" But she didn't say it because it really wasn't funny. Actually, when she thought about it, nothing was funny.

Ben heated her a can of soup and made some tea. She watched him as if he were a stranger, this grown man whose bottom she used to wipe, now fussing over her, his mother, this sad little woman Eleanor didn't recognize at all.

He began coming by every day to look in on her. One day he brought a flyer. "I Need a Good Home," it read over a photo of a skinny cat missing half of one ear and named, according to the block-printed caption, "Lucky."

"What the hell is this?" said Eleanor.

"Easy, Ma," said Ben, taking it from her and tossing it in the trash. "I saw it in the lobby and thought you could use a laugh. Obviously I was mistaken."

Later that afternoon Myra stopped by. Eleanor listened politely as she kvetched about the Boulder senior social scene. "Honestly, Ellie, the way some women throw themselves at men! Cooking on the first date. Doing his laundry. Even vacuuming!" But all Eleanor could think about was that stupid cat. What was his name again?

As soon as Myra left, Eleanor fished the flyer out of the trash. "Lucky." Judging by the photo, he was anything but. Against her better judgement Eleanor picked up the phone. Before she knew it she was walking back from a neighboring unit with a cardboard box in her arms.

Once inside, she set the box on the floor. Lucky crept out and sniffed the air. He slunk around the perimeter of the living room, finally stopping behind the sofa. Eleanor crouched and called to him. He stared at her, his eyes wide. She reached out a hand. He hissed at her.

"Fine," she said, leaving him where he was. When it was time for bed, Eleanor put out some water and a saucer of milk, planning to take the poor thing back in the morning.

Sometime in the night Eleanor woke to find a pair of eyes staring at her from the foot of the bed. She sat up slowly and extended her hand. Lucky tensed. Eleanor froze. Eyes locked, each waited for the other to make a move.

Finally, Lucky leaned his head forward and nuzzled Eleanor's hand. Soon he was letting her pet him, and soon after that he was purring in her arms.

"You're not so tough, are you?" she whispered. "You're not so tough at all."

The next day when Ben came by, he spied the empty saucer on the floor. "What's going on, Ma?" he said. "Don't tell me you went and got Lucky last night."

"That's a rather personal question, don't you think?" she said, a small smile coming to her face.

Hey, hey, ho, ho

Richard went most days without talking to a soul. Sometimes he went weeks or even months. A two-room cabin in the middle of 50-odd wooded acres constituted his entire world, not counting occasional trips down into Boulder for supplies — and even more occasionally to visit Dorothy. It was a life as carefully controlled as the man who had constructed it.

And now both control and man were breaking down.

"You look like shit," said Dorothy, opening her door to him. He walked silently inside. She shut the door and joined him on the couch. "Are you sleeping?"

He shook his head, no.

"Drinking?"

"Not so far."

She nodded, and for the first time in weeks he felt able to breathe.

They had met in '91 when a DUI landed Richard in the Sunday night AA meeting Dorothy had been attending for years. Upon first sight, each recognized the other — if not as individuals, then for the cliches they represented: haunted Viet vet and graying hippie chick. Instant dislike gradually softened to tolerance and eventually to grudging acceptance. Finally, one night in December, he rang her doorbell and they became lovers.

That first night she had run her hands over his body, stopping only when she came to the hole in his left bicep. It was a ragged inch in diameter and extended twice as deep into the meat of his arm.

"Go ahead," he whispered.

She put her finger inside, feeling the knots of scar tissue lining the obscene indentation. "Does it hurt?"

He shrugged. "There's some muscle and nerve damage that gives me trouble," he said, flexing his hand. "Other than that, it's just your basic flesh wound." That was as much as he'd ever said about his war experience, but she hadn't needed a degree in psychology to know that the hole in his flesh represented the least of his wounds.

Dorothy watched him now, leaning forward on her couch, his body coiled, his hands clenched on his thighs. "If we're going to do this," he said, "let's do it."

They rode to Denver in silence, taking 36 to 25 to Spear to Colfax. At the corner of Bannock they saw the first sign: "Say No to War!" Dorothy honked and the sign holder gave her a thumbs up. They passed the beginnings of a crowd in front of the City and County Building. A block beyond, they found an open meter and parked. Richard stood stiffly beside the car, taking in the air of chaos, the people streaming by, the honking horns and raised voices. It brought back his only previous experience at a demonstration — which had involved being spat on and called "baby killer."

"You going to be all right?" said Dorothy.

"Too soon to tell."

They found a spot on the edge of the gathering and listened to the speakers taking turns at the microphone. The atmosphere was half political rally, half carnival. There were an abundance of hand-made signs, outlandish costumes and black balloons.

Just before noon, the crowd formed into a ragged line. Mounted cops watched impassively as the marchers walked 16th street to the Adam's Mark where the President was supposedly speaking for $1,000 a plate. Along the way, the first chant broke out: "No War for Votes! No War for Oil!" Beside her, Dorothy felt Richard flinch at a sudden noise overhead. She looked up to see a helicopter circling low.

"Easy, cowboy," she said softly.

The chanting grew in intensity as the marchers reached the metal barricades in front of the hotel. On the other side a phalanx of city cops scanned the crowd from behind their mirror shades. Beside them news cams panned and zoomed, searching out color and motion.

"Hey, hey, ho, ho!" someone yelled. "Your war machine has got to go!" The rest of the crowd picked up the chant. Richard winced at the childishness of the words. Suddenly he realized coming here was a mistake. What the hell had he hoped to accomplish? Exorcise old demons? Single-handedly stop the nation from sliding into insanity? Save another generation of young men and women from spilling their innocence on foreign soil?

"Hey, hey, ho, ho!" the chant grew louder around Richard. Just as he was about to turn and fight his way back through the crowd, something made him glance up. In the hotel windows, people with name tags on their lapels and drinks in their hands stared down in amusement at the sideshow below them. A rage gripped Richard, a fierce desire to pierce each smirk with a high velocity round. To literally wipe the smiles off their faces. He knew this rage like an old companion — knew he could take it home and let it feed on him. Or he could stand and do what he'd come to do.

"Hey, hey, ho, ho!" he yelled in the most unnatural act of his life, an absurd leap of faith, a desperate prayer that his voice would somehow make a difference.

Let go

"Tom, take a walk with me." Tom looked up from his monitor to find Milo standing behind him. Before Tom could say anything, Milo turned and headed out of the small office. Tom, puzzled by his boss's behavior, followed him out into the hall and back to the rear door of the building. It opened onto a metal stairway overlooking the alley.

Milo lit a cigarette and leaned his arms on the railing. Tom waited for him to speak. Milo stared off toward the foothills. "I'm sorry," he said finally, handing Tom an envelope. "It's nothing you did. Hell, you're the hardest worker I've ever met."

"But —, " Tom stammered. "Jill's pregnant. I need this job."

"I feel like shit. If there was any other way..." Milo shrugged and headed back inside.

Ten minutes later Tom stood in the alley, his arms around a cardboard box of his personal possessions. He couldn't think. He couldn't breathe. What was he going to say to Jill? How could this have happened to him? What was he going to do?

He threw up the remains of his lunch into the cardboard box.

After that, he spent the next couple of hours driving aimlessly around Boulder. It was a shock to see all the people still going about their lives as if nothing had happened. The guy in spandex riding a Gitane. The CU students weaving their way through the Broadway traffic. The homeless guy on the median — wait a minute. The guy's face seemed uncomfortably familiar. Hadn't Tom met him last Summer at a Web Designers and Developers meeting?

Tom was only a couple of blocks from home now. Instead he turned west on Baseline and drove up Flagstaff. He climbed the winding road and pulled off at Panorama Point. He got out of the car and walked onto the overlook. He felt lightheaded, grabbing the wooden railing to steady himself.

"Just got the news?" said a voice at his elbow. He turned to find a young guy in a Spike and Mike T-shirt.

"The first day's the hardest," said a voice at Tom's other elbow. This one belonged to a guy with a crew cut, a bushy goatee and two hoops through his ear.

"Designer or developer?" said the first guy.

"Web programmer," said Tom.

"I did C++," said the goatee guy. "For a start-up. Five million initial capitalization to develop a digital paperclip. The founder walked away with two mil. I got a mouse pad with the company logo."

"I worked in Flash," said the T-shirt guy somewhat defensively.

They all stood silently for a while, looking down on Boulder.

"When I got the news," said Goatee, "I came up here to jump. But it's not a long enough drop. You can't be sure it'll finish you. More likely you'll just break some bones. And without a health plan where would that leave you?"

Tom shuddered and gripped the railing. T-shirt looked down at Tom's left hand. "Uh oh," he said. "He's got a wedding ring."

"Shit," said Goatee softly, putting a sympathetic hand on Tom's shoulder.

"Working up the courage to go home and tell her?" said T-shirt. Tom nodded his head. T-shirt nodded in sympathy. "My old lady was really understanding when I told her. She was great, man. Behind me 100 percent. 'It's not your fault. We'll get through this together.' Really made me feel good. Till the 'let go' test."

"The 'let go' test?" said Tom.

"It's how you tell if she's really behind you," said Goatee. "You tell her the news, she gives you the big hug, and if you let go first, you're Okay — she means it. If she lets go first..."

"Mine kicked me out three weeks later," said T-shirt.

The three of them stood silently again.

Goatee checked his watch. "I gotta get going. My shift starts in 15 minutes." He reached into a pocket and pulled out a Home Depot nametag.

"I'm outa here, too," said T-shirt, pulling on a Chili's cap.

"Good luck, man," said Goatee. "If you need company, someone's up here most days. Looking out over the beautiful town we used to rule."

Tom drove home, doing his best to put the two guys out of his mind. He pulled up at the house, took a deep breath and got out of the car. Inside, Jill came up to him, wearing a big smile and a new maternity dress.

"What do you think?" she said, spinning for him.

"I got laid off," Tom blurted out.

Jill's hand went to her mouth. Then she reached for him. "Oh, baby, I'm so sorry," she said.

Tom relaxed into the hug, feeling safe and warm for the first time that awful day. Then, just before he could pull away, Jill let go.

Jam

Vicki was late and traffic wasn't moving. She glared in helpless fury at the brake lights in front of her, then at the dashboard clock.

3:05. Damn.

"Jamie got jelly on the window," sing-sang a voice from the back seat.

"I sowwy," chirped another, younger voice.

Vicki looked in the mirror. Caitlyn, Vicki's 5-year-old, was pointing across at her stepbrother Jamie, whose little round face was splotched with strawberry jam. Beside him on the window were two perfect, jam-colored handprints.

"Don't touch anything else until we get to Margaret's," Vicki said to his reflection in the mirror. "Okay?"

"Otay."

He actually said, "Otay." Just like that Little Rascal. It was cute and heartbreaking at the same time. Jamie was three and suffered from a speech delay. That's where they were going now — to Margaret, the speech therapist, for Jamie's 3 o' clock appointment. Vicki glanced at the dash.

3:07. Damn.

Vicki had left extra early today, figuring that Broadway would be slow. But apparently not early enough. Every time she drove, it seemed the traffic was worse — and Vicki drove a lot. As wife and mother, she was the designated driver for her family. Her blended family. She'd always hated the term, but now she had to admit that yes, in fact, she did feel like she was living in a blender — constantly spinning around, slamming into walls, trying desperately not to be chopped to pieces. And at the controls was Chuck's ex, The Witch.

"I see mo'cycle!" chimed Jamie as a Harley nosed into the lane in front of Vicki.

"Motorcycle," corrected Caitlyn in her 5-year-old, superior voice.

"Mo'cycle," repeated Jamie happily. He met Vicki's eyes in the mirror and gave her a wide, jam-smeared smile. God, but he was adorable. Just like his daddy, Chuck. Nice-Guy Chuck. Walk-All-Over-Me Chuck. Take-the-House-and-the-Range-Rover-and-a-Thousand-a-Month-in-Child-Support Chuck. The only thing the poor man had stood up for was shared custody of Jamie. So of course, The Witch had since dedicated herself to a single goal: getting the agreement overturned. She grilled poor Jamie after each visit for every skinned knee, every raised voice, anything she could use to portray Chuck and Vicki as unfit parents and grab sole custody for herself.

The Harley's brake lights flashed off, and traffic began to move. Vicki snuck a peek at the dash.

3:11.

With luck, maybe they could make it by 3:15. Please, God. Margaret's policy was clear. Twenty minutes late and the session was canceled. And wouldn't that just make The Witch's day?

"Pee yew," said Caitlyn. "The air stinks."

"Stin's," repeated Jamie.

It did smell of diesel fumes. Vicki checked the air intake button. Her fingers came away sticky. "Jamie," she said, keeping her voice calm, "when we were leaving the house and I told you to go directly to your car seat, did you climb in the front first?"

"I sowwy," he said softly.

Vicki choked down the angry words that welled up. Why give The Witch more ammo? She glanced at the dash again.

3:14. Damn, damn, damn.

Traffic inched forward, and Vicki saw the "Lane Closed Ahead" sign. She leaned her head against the steering wheel. How could she have been so stupid as to forget the big construction project was finally beginning this week?

When she sat back upright, her forehead came away from the steering wheel sticky.

"I sowwy," came Jamie's voice from the back seat.

Vicki rubbed jam off her forehead and tried to think. The next intersection was College. If she turned left, she could cut over to 9th and bypass the construction. She looked left. A mud-encrusted Jeep filled the turn lane, with a dreadlocked dude at the wheel. He caught her eyes, saw the desperation there and gestured for her to cut in. She blew him a kiss and accelerated through the intersection.

She drove like a demon, squealing the turn onto 9th and past the graveyard. She caught every light and reached Broadway in minutes — just in time to find a Camry backing out of a parking space. She pulled in and shut off the engine. Then she looked at the dash: 3:21.

Vicki put her forearms on the sticky steering wheel, laid her head down and cried.

"I sowwy," Jamie wailed from the back seat. "Don' cwy. I sowwy."

Something in his voice made Vicki lift her head. Not exactly sure why, she reached for the dashboard clock — and found stickiness on the Time Set button. She grabbed her purse, pulled out her cell and looked at the time on its screen.

2:57.

Vicki popped loose her seat belt and turned in her seat. Jamie's eyes widened in confusion as she leaned over the seat back, cupped his cheeks and kissed his adorable, precious, sticky little face.

Lea

Lea's car, had she owned one, could easily have sported a "Colorado Native" bumper sticker. Her bloodlines went back so far they disappeared into history. Then again it wasn't her way to concern herself with something as meaningless as history. She accepted the newcomers as a fact of nature. She accepted their strange ways, their air of ownership over land that had been in her family for untold generations. Mostly she stayed out of their way, and the majority of them never even knew they were intruding on her. She accepted this, too, with an inhuman calmness.

That's not to say Lea didn't imagine killing them. She imagined it daily. Looking down on them as they ran past in their gaudy, unnatural colors, intent on their running trails, completely unaware of the larger world around them. How easy it would be to leap down on their backs, to sink her claws into their shoulders and her powerful jaws into their necks. With a quick shake of her head, she would break their necks and drag them into the underbrush to feed on at her leisure. But she never acted on these impulses — even with the young ones who'd be so easy to take.

Lea lived alone except when the madness of lust overtook her and then three months afterwards when she had young to nurture until they were old enough to leave home and stake out hunting grounds of their own. For food, she mostly hunted deer. They were plentiful and fat from wandering down to feed on the shrubs and flowers the newcomers so thoughtfully provided.

That's not to say things were perfect for Lea. It was almost two weeks since she had last fed and her belly ached from hunger. Deer were no easy prey. They could outrun her in the open. They were also very sensitive to their environment and thus difficult to surprise. For example, at this very moment Lea was sitting motionless on a rock outcropping above three young — and very edible — does. Her tawny coat blended perfectly with the rocks around her. She was downwind of the trio. Yet still something was spooking them. They bent to eat, then popped up, their eyes wide, their ears extended, their nostrils twitching, sampling the air for some clue to explain the unease that gripped them.

Lea watched patiently as the trio moved ever closer, their heads bobbing down, then back up, then down, then up again. Her breathing slowed as her muscles tensed. Her ears stood up and her tail twitched in anticipation. Her brain effortlessly calculated the precise trajectory to the nearest doe. She needed this kill. She was weak from hunger, lightheaded and clumsy. She would not survive much longer without feeding.

Just before she could leap, another creature burst onto the scene. Small and loud, it ran into view, making noises out of proportion to its size. The deer froze, heads swiveling in perfect synchrony. The creature froze as well, staring at the deer as they stared back at it.

From behind the small creature came one of the strange voices Lea had learned to associate with the newcomers: "Roscoe! Roscoe!"

The deer unfroze and leapt into the air, their legs springing them away. They bounded past Lea's perch at

full speed — and just out of reach. She leapt anyway, hitting the ground a few feet short of them. They wheeled away from her. She put on her maximum burst of speed.

Behind her the small creature sprang to life. Its annoying, high-pitched voice distracted her as she made a desperate plunge for the nearest doe. Her claws caught its flank, scraping down its smooth hide. It twisted out of her grasp. Lea fell in an ungainly heap as the deer bounded away, cheating her out of the meal she so desperately needed.

Lea turned and regained her feet, facing the intruder who had driven away her dinner.

"Roscoe, where are you?" The newcomer's voice was faint, distant. "Roscoe, come!" Lea tuned it out.

She focused her attention completely on the small animal in front of her. It faced her, paws splayed, ears back, mouth snarling. Then it grew quiet as if something in its tiny brain recognized the position it was in.

Lea's breathing slowed, her muscles tensed and her tail began to twitch.

After dark, Lea lay quietly, purring to herself. Her belly was full and hunger was a memory. She would sleep well tonight and awake to live another day — to run and hunt and lust and feel the sun on her skin.

Just before she dropped off to sleep she offered up a quiet prayer of gratitude to the universe — and to the newcomers who had provided her with such a timely and tasty meal.

Long, dark night

It was three in the morning, and sleep just wasn't happening. Jill rolled over on her back with a sigh. She lay, arms stiff by her side, eyes open, staring up into the darkness. Beside her, Tom interrupted his gentle snoring long enough to roll onto his side. His leg brushed hers. She jerked her leg away.

Tom's snore started up again. God, how could he sleep? Why was she the one awake and worrying when it was Tom who'd been laid off? She wanted to elbow him into consciousness and make him tell her how they were going to pay the mortgage this month — not to mention saving up for the baby that was going to be here in less than five months. Did he plan to have a new job by then? Or was he just going to go on like this forever, shrugging helplessly whenever she brought the subject up?

Stop it, Jill, just stop it. You're only making yourself sick. You know it's a difficult job market right now, especially for programmers. You know Tom is trying his best to find work. In fact, you know it's killing him to have to go begging every day, pleading with some stranger for an interview, a referral, a chance to provide for his family.

Like it wasn't killing her? Like she wasn't putting in full shifts at the ER, then riding the bus home, hoping against hope for a piece of good news? But day after day, she'd open the door, look in his face and find the same embarrassed helplessness there. God, she hated that look! Like he was some kind of wounded puppy for her to comfort. Well, who was comforting her? Who was reassuring her that things were going to be OK?

This isn't helping. Turning on each other is the one sure way not to get through tough times. Tom needs your support just like he needs his sleep.

Did he really? Or maybe what he really needed was to feel more anxiety instead of less. Maybe he needed something to light a fire under him. Maybe he needed less support from her. Less sympathy. Less coddling. Maybe she should kick him awake right now and demand he get his ass out of bed and not come back until he was employed again.

You don't really believe that. You know he's only trying to keep himself in balance and maintain a positive attitude instead of letting the situation overwhelm him.

Forget balance. They didn't need balance. They needed income. Or was Tom just planning on shrugging helplessly when collection agencies started hounding them? When the bank came to foreclose on the house? When the baby needed food? Clothes? Medicine?

Down, girl. Try to be fair.

Screw fair. Screw being Mrs. Nice. What Jill really wanted was for Tom to be strong. She wanted him to stop slinking around with his tail between his legs, politely asking the world to give him a job. Stop asking and start demanding. Make the world pay attention. Do whatever it took. Break the law if he had to. Jill wanted to know that he would rob a bank if that's what it took to provide for his family.

Now, there's a great idea! A man can really support his family from behind bars. Not to mention having a convict for your baby's father.

At least he'd be a man.

And you? What are you? A cold, selfish monster?

Better that than a spineless pushover.
Heartless shrew.
Doormat.
Nag.
Victim.
Bitch.
Jill took a mental deep breath, the two voices inside her falling silent. They waited like opposing attorneys leaving it to the judge to decide. The judge took her time, then whispered the verdict out loud to herself, "Two more weeks, and if the situation hasn't changed by then, I'll change it for him."

It was four in the morning and Jill was sleeping soundly. Beside her, yanked an hour before from a deep and dreamless sleep by the whispered sentence, Tom lay on his back, arms stiff by his side, eyes open, staring up into the darkness.

The green vest

Bobby was 10 when he saw the inside of McGuckin Hardware for the first time. It took his young breath away with its aisles and aisles of everything anyone could ever want in the world. Tools. Housewares. Paint and Accessories. Pet Supplies. Electrical. Sporting Goods. And, most wondrous of all — Nuts and Fasteners.

But even better than all the wonderful things for sale were the men in the green vests. They stood in the middle of the store, at the intersection of Broadway and Parkway, and waited for people to ask them questions. And then they answered them!

Bobby stood by his mother's side as she gave the nearest green-vested man one of those girlish smiles that made Bobby so embarrassed to watch. "Hi," she simpered in a syrupy voice, quite different from the one she used late at night when she was drunk and telling Bobby he was no better than his good-for-nothing father back in San Diego. "I was hoping you had a door knob. Something to replace the one on my new bedroom door."

"Follow me," said the man. They followed him to a whole aisle full of knobs. Bobby's mother fussed and dithered before finally choosing a simple brass one.

"I don't suppose I could offer you a few dollars to come help me install it?" she continued, making Bobby blush with shame.

"Sorry, ma'am," said the man. He turned to Bobby. "But I can teach this fine young man here what to do, and I'm sure he'll have no problem taking care of it for you."

Bobby never forgot that moment. Long after his mother had lost her looks, and then her life, to the bottle. Long after a lawyer showed up to tell Bobby his father had died and left him a substantial trust fund. Long after Bobby had entered his twenties and then his thirties, his life settled into a comfortable and unchanging routine, Bobby still remembered that first, magic visit to McGuckin's.

Not that it was his last visit, not at all. Hardly a month went by that Bobby didn't make at least one trip to buy something he didn't need, such as the High-Output Evaporative Humidifier or the 1/2" Magnum Hammer-Drill or the 25 feet of 7/8" High-Pressure Braided PVC Tubing. It didn't really matter. What mattered was the precious opportunity to ask a man a question and get an answer.

One morning Bobby woke and knew he couldn't go on like this. He knew it was time for him to grow up and stop asking questions. It was time for him to answer questions. He considered applying to wear a green vest of his own, but he didn't think he was cut out for regular employment — showing up on time, following orders, and so on. So if they wouldn't give him a vest, he decided to make one for himself.

A little over a week later he emerged from his apartment. His back ached. His eyes were red from strain and lack of sleep. But in his hands he held his very own green vest. It was perfect, down to the row of white buttons that no one ever buttoned to the two pockets on the front with the white logo on the left one. Bobby had drawn it in white permanent marker in perfect detail from memory.

He rode the Hop to McGuckin's, the vest in a brown paper grocery bag on his lap. Once inside, he wandered through housewares to a quiet corner of the store. There he pulled the vest out of the bag and slipped it on.

His body tingled with excitement as he strolled down the aisle.

"Excuse me," said a voice behind him. Bobby turned to find a young mother and son.

"Yes, ma'am?" he said.

"We're looking for door knobs?"

"Follow me." Bobby led them across the center of the store, walking confidently and glancing over his shoulder. "That's a fine young man you've got with you. I bet he'll be a great help installing the door knob on your bedroom door."

The young mother gave Bobby a funny look, but he felt too lightheaded and glorious to notice as he led them to the door knob aisle.

"Here you go," he said, glancing at the name tag on the first green vest he found there. "Pete will be glad to help you." Bobby handed them off to another green-vested young man and strolled away through the center of the store to the nearest exit. "Have a good one," he called to the blue-vested cashier as he strolled past.

Once outside, he stopped and sucked in a deep breath, deeper than he'd ever breathed before, and as he exhaled, he sighed strong and low.

The sound of his sigh as it reached his ears, a sound he had never heard himself make before, was the sigh of a man.

Chop wood

Richard woke slowly to thin slivers of dawn-red light piercing the cabin windows. He gave his mind time to reenter his body, feeling every one of his 52 years, before pushing himself upright and then out of the narrow cot he called bed. The plank floor was cold beneath his bare feet as he padded into the front room to stoke the wood stove and put water on for coffee. Glancing out the window, he caught a dark shape slumped on the porch. He opened the door and stepped out into the cold.

"I gather things didn't go too well," he said to Dorothy, now recognizable in her navy peacoat and watch cap. She stared off into the dim light of the early morning, not speaking. After a moment he spoke again, "Come in and get warm." He waited patiently as she pulled herself to her feet, stamped those feet to return circulation and then finally brushed past him into the cabin. By then the kettle was whistling, so he took it off the stove and made coffee for them both. "How bad was it?"

She slumped in his ancient rocking chair, blowing on the mug he handed her. "We lost the Senate."

"Damn."

"But hey," she continued brightly, "we swept the local elections, so our little liberal enclave remains intact. And there's always 'West Wing.' I guess I can learn to shut out the rest of the world. Like you."

Richard took his seat on the faded armchair and drank his coffee as the sun rose slowly over the evergreens that sheltered the cabin. After a while, Dorothy slipped off her coat and cap and stared out the window.

"You want to talk about it?" he asked her.

"Not particularly. It'll just get me upset all over again." He nodded and got up to pour them both some more coffee. "I suppose I should be grown up about this," she continued. "It's only politics, right? Just a big game. So our side lost. We'll get 'em next time." She accepted a fresh cup from him. "But it's not just a game. It has consequences. Real things will happen because of this. Real people will hurt. Children will go hungry. Poor families will have it even harder than they already do. And kids will die to make the world safe for big oil. Shit, shit, shit." She shook her head. "If I keep talking like this, I'm going to lose it. I mean really lose it."

She looked up, and he saw the haunted look in her eyes. In answer, he stood and put on his coat and boots. He opened the door and stepped outside. She set down her coffee and, grabbing her coat and cap, headed out after him. Together they walked about a hundred yards to a small shed which Richard opened. He took out a large axe and held it out to her. She raised her eyebrows. He kept the axe and walked over to a large stump with a pile of cut wood beside it. As she watched, he put a piece of wood on the stump, lifted the axe above his head and brought it down, splitting the wood clean in two. He held out the axe. This time she took it from him.

He went about his day, carrying out the long list of chores he had planned for himself. Throughout, he heard the steady thwock of the axe striking wood. At noon he brought out a glass of cider and a bowl of chili and set it on a log near her. A couple of hours later the food was untouched, so he took it away without comment.

An hour before sunset, he crossed the yard and picked up an armload of split wood. She ignored him. Her arms were shaking with fatigue and there was blood on the axe handle from blisters that had formed and burst. He carried the wood inside.

Richard made two more trips, ferrying wood inside the cabin. On the third, he stopped beside Dorothy and took the axe from her trembling hands. He led her inside and silently undressed her. Beside the roaring wood stove was a large galvanized tub full of steaming water. Dorothy climbed in. Richard bathed her tenderly, applying salve to her blistered hands and wrapping them in gauze.

When he was finished, he lifted her from the tub, toweled her off and carried her into his bedroom. He laid her on the cot and wrapped her in quilts. She drifted toward sleep almost immediately. Just before she was gone, he bent down and kissed her forehead.

"We'll get 'em next time," he whispered.

One big happy

A week after Tom started sleeping on the couch, Jill's entire family descended on them for the holidays. Jill moved Tom's pillow and blanket back into the bedroom. "This is just while they're here," she said. "Don't get any ideas."

Jill's brother Teddy was the first to arrive, in a cherry red Miata. "Jilly, what's gotten into you?" he said, rubbing her protruding belly. "Wait, don't answer that!" He gave Tom a lewd wink.

Sister Connie showed up next with her latest boyfriend in tow. "This is Wayne. He's a doctor."

The parental Winnebago pulled into the driveway last. Mom hugged everyone while Dad ran a thick, yellow extension cord up the driveway and through the living room window. "Where's your 220?" he said to Tom.

After assigning Teddy to the living room couch and Connie and Wayne to an inflatable mattress in the future nursery, the women congregated in the kitchen to plan the next day's big meal while the men hunkered in front of the TV.

"Is this all the channels you get?" said Teddy, thumbing the remote. "I have digital cable myself — sports package, movie package, the whole enchilada."

"How's your work?" said Jill's dad. "You should think about taking on a second job while Jill's on maternity leave."

Doctor Wayne sniffed the air. "Do I smell cat urine?"

Dinner was free-range chicken piccata. Connie and Wayne abstained. "Since when are you a vegetarian?" Jill said to Connie.

"Since I moved to Berkeley. The real People's Republic."

"What a bitch," said Jill when she and Tom were alone in the bedroom. "'This is Wayne. He's a doctor.' You didn't tell anyone you're out of work, did you?"

"Actually I don't think I've said one word since they got here."

"Good."

The next morning over breakfast Jill handed everyone the list of sights she'd prepared so they could all get to know the "real Boulder."

"All I want to see is the Ramsey house," said Mom.

"Just point Wayne and me to the nearest Trader Joe's," said Connie. "Oh wait, you don't have Trader Joe's here, do you?"

"I'll hit the Mall myself," said Teddy. "That nice new one I saw on the way into town."

The family scattered to their various destinations, leaving Jill to fume. Tom made the mistake of trying to soothe her. "Everybody's family is a little nuts."

"Why don't you get your own life in order first — starting with a job," she said. "Then you can criticize my family."

By the time the big meal arrived, Tom was a mess. He felt like the silent eye in the middle of a familial hurricane of blustering boasts, catty remarks and cutting jokes. Eventually everyone seemed to notice he wasn't speaking — or eating for that matter. They continued with their eating and bantering. But when Tom continued sitting there in silence, one by one they fell silent, too.

"Is something wrong, Tom?" said Mom finally.

"No," said Jill.

"Actually," said Tom, "I got fired three months ago and I've taken over $10,000 in cash advances on my credit cards just to pay bills." Jill stared daggers at him, but he went on. "Last week Jill threw me out of the bedroom and if I don't find work soon, she'll no doubt throw me out of the house."

No one said anything for a long while. Then Teddy spoke up. "$10,000?" he said. "Hell, I've got over $50,000 in debts. They foreclosed on my condo last month and they'll be repossessing the Miata any day now."

"Wayne's not really a doctor," said Connie. "He's an acupuncturist. Or he would be if he had any clients."

"As long as we're baring our souls," Mom piped in, "your father drinks too much, I can't stop playing the lottery and we haven't had sex in over 10 years."

That night while the women were cleaning up, Jill's dad pulled Tom aside. "My little girl can be a real handful. Gets it from her mother. When they were passing out the sensitivity gene, both those women were off shopping or something." He shook his head. "I wouldn't blame you if you washed your hands of her. But — hang in there, Okay? Underneath the hard shell, she's just a scared kid about to have a kid of her own." He took out a check and pressed it into Tom's hand.

Tom reflexively tried to hand it back.

"Take it," insisted Dad. "Use it for marriage therapy if you have to. Just please don't give up on Jill." He put a hand on Tom's shoulder. "Or I swear to God I'll pack up my entire family, track you down in the Winnebago and make you have dinner with us over and over again."

The Famous Writer loses it

Celia brought the brochure to the Tuesday night writer's group. "$95 is a lot of money for a one-day seminar," said Jenny, who specialized in semi-autobiographical short stories.

"There's a $15 discount for early registration," said Toby, who wrote travel articles and nature poetry.

"Still, that's a whole weekend's worth of tips," said Stella — science fiction and fantasy novels.

"The question is: are we serious about being writers or not?" said Mickey — Christian screenplays.

"I'm going," said Celia — journals of her personal battle with colon cancer.

Saturday morning the Famous Writer greeted them at the door to the rundown motel conference room just off 28th. Celia thought she caught a whiff of liquor on his breath. At 8 in the morning! She found a seat in the back next to a woman name-tagged "Greta" who whispered, "Have you heard him speak before? He's really good. Very inspirational."

Celia studied him at his post by the door. He was shorter than she'd expected, and older. She took out her notebook and began jotting a description. He wore a threadbare navy blazer and faded jeans. His cowboy boots were scuffed. His smile seemed practiced — even though it never quite made it up to his eyes. Celia was especially proud of that observation.

Soon the Famous Writer strode to the front of the

room and clipped on a wireless mike. "Before we begin," he said, "let's take a moment to go around and share why you each want to write. Anyone?"

"To express myself," said a young woman. The Famous Writer nodded politely and said "Um."

"To offer hope and inspiration to others," said an older woman. Before the Famous Writer could "um" again, a snort came from a corner of the room. Everyone followed the sound to find a young man entirely in black. The Famous Writer walked over and stood in front of him.

"And why, pray tell, are you here?"

"Me," shrugged the young man, "I want to live the writer's lifestyle."

"The writer's lifestyle?" repeated the Famous Writer, his smile straining. And this time, observed Celia, not only did his eyes not partake of his smile, they seemed to be twitching uncontrollably. "And what exactly would that be? Owing thousands in student loans for a useless M.A.? Or maybe it's having the Times Book Review call your second novel 'a true gem' only to be dropped by your agent because you're not selling through? Or how about driving around the country conducting idiotic seminars for brainless, self-deluded amateurs?"

The room was alive with electricity. The Famous Writer turned around for a second, and Celia thought she saw him sneak a sip from a small bottle. She jotted the detail down.

"Stop writing!" Celia looked up from her notepad to find the Famous Writer standing over her. "I mean it. Put the pen down or I'll shove it in your ear."

Celia stuffed her pen into her purse.

"All of you. Stop writing. Get on with your lives. If you love great literature, for God's sake, read it and be

properly humbled. Stop destroying things for the handful of real writers in the world. Architects don't have to
compete with a million amateurs drawing up blueprints! Dentists don't have to deal with wannabes will-
ing to work for free copies of the x-rays!" He was drinking openly now, not bothering to hide the bottle of
cheap peppermint schnapps. "Writing is not therapy,
people. It doesn't make you a better person. It does not
make you feel better about yourself — not if you're
doing it right."

Despite herself, Celia fished her pen out of her purse
and began writing again. The Famous Writer froze in
mid-rant, spun and grabbed the pen out of her hand.
"For the love of God, haven't you heard a word I've
said?" His eyes bulged. His breath came in rasps. "Get
out of here! All of you! Go fall in love. Play sports.
Develop a drug habit if that's what it takes. Just don't
write another word unless you're the one-in-a-literal-
million whose very life depends on it! Unless your
heart would stop beating and your brain explode. Then
and only then do you have the right to write!"

The Famous Writer collapsed in a heap on the floor.
The room was utterly silent at first, then someone
began to clap. One by one, the rest of the room joined
in until they were all on their feet, applauding loudly.

"Didn't I tell you," said Greta to Celia. "Isn't he wonderful?"

Deep cover

Jake stopped at the overlook to give his pickup for one last going-over. No stickers on the bumper. No tracts behind the seats. No spent cartridges on the floor. He was good to go.

He descended into enemy territory, his senses on full alert. He would need all his wits about him to fulfill his mission and escape detection. Again he felt the flush of pride just knowing the Brigade had trusted him with something so important to the Cause. He would not fail them.

Jake drove carefully, studying everything around him. So this was it. The center of the Conspiracy. The outpost of the traitorous One World Government. Ground Zero for the coming Holy War. He kept his eyes peeled for foreign cars, government agents, racial intermingling — anything to include in his first transmission back.

After reconnoitering for almost two hours, he stopped at the cheapest looking motel he could find. Inside, he forced himself to smile at the Mex behind the counter. "How much for a room?" he said. "Go back to your own stinking country and stop taking work from decent white people," he didn't say.

When the guy quoted him a rate, Jake was sure he was being cheated. No room in Montana had ever cost that much. But, remembering his covert training, he just nodded and counted the bills out of his wallet.

After throwing his duffel on the bed of his room, Jake unpacked the disposable camera and headed back out in his pickup. He snapped shots of the NIST building, laughing to himself at the ridiculous notion that anyone would believe such a large complex was devoted to "Standards and Technology." When he followed the signs up to NCAR, he laughed even harder at the poor fools below who believed this stone fortress overlooking them was conducting "Atmospheric Research."

On his way back down and then north to downtown, Jake did have to admit the Shadow Government was clever. Just look how they kept the dark-skinned agents under cover so that the only people visible on the streets were white.

He found an open meter at the west end of a street called Pearl where an unusually large stream of people were on foot. Jake nonchalantly joined the flow. Hearing the sounds of drums up ahead, he slipped out his disposable camera. Within a block he had come upon a scene of shocking depravity: youths with tangled hair, beating tribal drums and writhing like savages. Beside them were other youths with backpacks and sleeping rolls. Obviously fresh recruits for the Global Army, drawn by the hypnotic jungle beat.

The only other detail Jake found to include in his report was a series of so-called "Art Galleries" featuring coded visual messages. Jake couldn't say what exactly the visual messages were; he just knew them when he saw them.

It was a few blocks south of Pearl Street that Jake made his big discovery. Standing by itself a block east of Broadway was a bizarre, foreign-looking building. He snapped a few shots from across the street, then wandered over to join the people walking in and out.

Inside, his heart stopped in his chest. Every inch of

every wall was covered with Arab markings like nothing he had ever seen before. And in the corners of the room there weren't even chairs — only pillows on the floor like some Oriental bawdy house. This was not America, this "Dushanbe Teahouse." This hotbed of betrayal and accommodation. He snapped pictures of all the people at the tables. Now, the world would finally have to see. There was no war on terror. The terrorists and government agents sat together drinking tea and plotting to take away our guns and murder unborn white babies.

"Excuse me," said a black-dressed waiter. "Please don't take pictures in here." Jake pushed the man's arm away and continued his work. "Please. You're making everyone very uncomfortable." Jake finished the rest of the reel. Everyone was staring at him by now. "Don't make me call the police, sir."

Jake turned and ran out of the room before the Storm Troopers could arrive. He fled through the darkened park and to his pickup. He pulled out into traffic and headed for the motel.

There was some kind of jam-up and the traffic wasn't moving at all. He pounded the steering wheel. He had to get to ground before the Black Helicopters found him with the evidence in his camera. The brake lights went off ahead of him and traffic eased forward half a block, then froze again. Dammit! He had to transmit his shocking truth. He had to let the world know that Boulder was the center of unspeakable evil. The staging ground for the betrayal of everything American.

And the traffic was terrible.

Finding Dr. Right

Face it, Tom," said Jill over breakfast one morning. "If we're going to make it, we need professional help."

"Okay," said Tom.

"You're not going to argue with me?"

"I saved the Monday paper. It has a directory of therapists."

"Well," said Jill, taken aback. "I brought home the latest copy of Nexus."

"Great," said Tom. "Now all we have to do is find someone we can both agree on."

By unspoken agreement they went to neutral corners to prepare their cases. An hour later they returned to the table. "You go first," said Tom.

"No, you," said Jill.

"Okay," said Tom. "I've found a couple of options. Both are licensed psychologists with extensive experience in couples' counseling."

"Do they have anything else in common?" said Jill. "Such as, perhaps — a penis?"

"They do, in fact, happen to be men. But that's beside the point — "

"No, I think it's exactly the point. You want some old-school, tight-ass Freudian type who will see everything your way and label me an overemotional, castrating bitch."

"Not at all, Jill."

87

"Good. Then you won't have any objection to," Jill read from the Nexus, "'a soul-centered spirit guide who is familiar with traditional Western therapeutic modalities but who can also offer holistic options such as EMDR, dreamwork and Shamanic Journeys.'"

Tom held out his hand. Jill handed him the issue. "'Heart Speaker Spirit Angel, M.A.?'" he read. "Is this a joke?"

"There you go. Slamming the door again with your negative attitude."

"How come it's a negative attitude if I question your choice, but not when you question mine?"

"If you don't understand the difference, Tom," she said, throwing up her hands and storming out of the room, "then I can't explain it to you."

He stared after her, biting down on the angry words he knew would only be kerosene on the fire. He set down the Nexus and headed outside. Needing to do something with his hands, he decided to change the oil on the Corolla. He had just unscrewed the oil filter when he heard a voice coming from the direction of his feet.

"Hey there, neighbor!"

Shit. It must be the big, hairy guy from across the street. Tom had been avoiding him ever since he and Jill had moved in. So far Tom had limited contact to a few waves from driveway to driveway and a couple of shouted "Beautiful mornings!" But it looked like this just wasn't Tom's day. He slid out from under the Corolla and forced a smile onto his face. "Hello," he said.

"Changing the old oil, I see," said Mr. Big and Hairy.

"Yeah," said Tom.

"If I'm not mistaken, you changed it just three weeks ago and that means you're either anal-compulsive — "

"Or maybe I don't want to be inside right now," said Tom, completely surprising himself.

"Ouch," said the neighbor. "I know what that's like. Me and the old lady had a rough patch a few years back. We'd've been toast if it weren't for Dr. Julie."

"Dr. Julie?" said Jill later that afternoon. "No way am I calling a therapist on the recommendation of a man with hair in his ears."

"Fine," said Tom, picking up the phone. "I'll call." Jill glared at him as he dialed, then put his hand over the receiver. "Machine," he said, waiting for the beep. "Hello, we were referred to you by our neighbor. Could you please call us back and let us know about your credentials, such as are you a licensed psychologist? How many years have you been practicing? Do you offer a sliding scale?"

Jill grabbed the phone from him. "Can you do breath work or NLP?"

Tom grabbed the phone back. "Do you have a Ph.D?"

Jill grabbed it back again. "Enneagram?"

Tom was grabbing it back again when Dr. Julie came on the line. "Enough!" she said in a rich contralto. "I could hear you two from the next room. How about tomorrow at 10:00? I have a cancellation."

"Well, " said Tom.

"We haven't decided, " said Jill.

"Let me simplify your decision," said Dr. Julie "You can continue jockeying for someone to take your side against your partner or you can try me. I promise to be equally hard on both of you and to personally call your partner on every single attempt to shade the truth, shift the blame or otherwise justify their cruel, selfish and childlike behavior."

"We'll be there!" shouted Jill and Tom in unison.

Baby

The worse Bush and his team of clowns screwed up the economy, the better it was for Jeff. In over twenty years as a mortgage broker, he had never seen so many people so desperate to refinance their mortgages and pay off their maxed-out credit cards. It was a golden opportunity that might never come again. But try and tell that to his wife Linda.

"You have a daughter, Jeff, who barely even knows your face."

"I can't turn away business."

"You can damn well spend one Saturday afternoon with your own child. Besides, my book club has matinee tickets to the Denver Center."

And that's how Jeff ended up in the basement playroom of his Palo Park scrape-off with his not-quite-three-year-old daughter Claire. "What do you want to do?" he said.

"Tea party," she said.

Great. He checked his watch. Four more hours before Linda got back.

"Here," said Claire, handing him a red vinyl cup and saucer. "You sit down." Jeff sat in a child-sized white lacquer chair from Children's IKEA, his knees scraping his chin. Claire took a seat across from him, smoothing the front of her Baby Gap pink stretch cord jumper. "Drink," she commanded as she pretended to sip from her own cup, slurping loudly.

"I'm drinking," he said, putting the cup to his mouth.

"You don't do it right," she said and glared at him in a picture-perfect replica of Linda's most scathing look. Jeff glared back at Claire. With a swipe of her little arm, she knocked half the dishes off onto the floor. Jeff put down his cup and knocked the rest of the dishes off.

Claire stood, walked over to the shelves, pulled out a basket of dolls and dumped them on the floor. Jeff stood, followed her to the shelves and dumped out a basket of blocks. They both stood looking at each other. Claire knelt, reached onto the bottom shelf and produced a pink rubber ball. She cocked her arm and let the ball fly. It bounced off the wall, hit a nearby rocking chair and careened into Jeff's cheek.

"Ow!" he said. Claire put a hand to her mouth. Jeff rubbed his cheek. "That hurt," he said.

"Baby," she said to him.

"What did you say?"

"You're a baby."

He picked up the ball and threw it at the corner. It bounced off three walls and the dollhouse before smacking into Claire's leg. Jeff stared at her in horror. She rubbed her leg, her eyes wide. But she didn't cry.

"Wow," said Jeff. "You're a brave little girl."

"You're a baby," she repeated.

"Am not," he said, sticking out his tongue at her.

She giggled and stuck her tongue out at him. He lifted his hands in the air and contorted his face. Growling, he took a step toward her. She shrieked with laughter and ran away from him. He chased her around the playroom.

She ran behind the rocker. He crouched, growling as she giggled. He feinted left, then lunged right and caught her in his arms. They fell in a heap on the floor.

Jeff tickled her tummy and she laughed and laughed. Suddenly, she froze, a horrified look on her face.

"What's wrong?" Jeff said. Then he noticed the yellow puddle spreading beneath her. "Ha ha!" he taunted. "Who's the baby now?"

Claire burst into tears and pushed him away. Before he could stop her, she disappeared under the futon sofa. Jeff sat in the middle of the room, feeling like a total brute.

"Come on out," he said. "I'm sorry." Claire just wailed louder. Jeff looked down at the pee stain forming on the carpet. "Shit," he said under his breath and went to look for some carpet cleaner. When he got back, she had stopped wailing and was now whimpering softly. He lay down beside the futon. Claire was curled up, facing the wall.

"I'm sorry, Claire," he said. "You're not a baby." He took a deep breath. "If anyone's a baby here, it's me." She fell silent. "That's right," he continued. "I'm a big, stupid — " With each word she rolled a little more in his direction. " — stinky, poopie-face — " She was facing him now, hands over her mouth. " — baby!" She burst into delighted giggles.

When Linda came home a few hours later, she was astonished to find Jeff and Claire (dressed now in a blue snowflake jumper) bouncing a ball back and forth.

"How was the matinee?" said Jeff.

"Fine," answered Linda, slipping off her shoes. "But my feet are killing me," she said.

Jeff gave Claire a conspiratorial glance. "Baby," they whispered to each other.

The grace of Todd

Todd was working on a chicken fajita burrito outside Chipotle's on the Mall. "Did you hear they outlawed begging in Boulder?" he said.

"About time," muttered Zeke, his frat buddy, stuffing the last half of his steak burrito into his mouth.

A homeless guy leaned across the railing. "Hey, buddy, you gonna finish that?"

Todd hawked up a big one, and spit it on the remains of his burrito.

"Asshole," said the homeless guy.

"Get a job," said Todd.

"You owe me $8.50," said Zeke on the drive back to the frat house.

"I'll have to catch you later," said Todd. "I'm still waiting for this month's check from my dad."

"Not cool, dude. You owe money to everybody in the house."

That night Todd had an inspiration. "Civil disobedience," he said apropos of nothing.

"What?" said Zeke.

"You know, Martin Luther King and that Gandhi dude. How it's okay to break a law if you don't like it."

"You don't like the new law?"

"I like it fine. But I got a radical idea to score some change and get you all off my back till my dad's check comes."

The next afternoon, Todd stepped onto the median

93

of Broadway and Euclid with a plastic bucket and a sign reading: "Shame on the City Council! Support the Homeless Defense Fund." The response was immediate and overwhelming. People honked, flashed thumbs up, and most importantly, dropped money in the bucket. By 3:00, Todd figured he had more than 200 bucks.

But that wasn't all. Some fraternity brothers happened by in a cherry red Camaro. Seeing Todd, they busted out laughing and handed him a Coors. "Thanks," he said. "This civil disobedience shit is thirsty work." From then on, whenever he finished a beer more frat boys always seemed to come along with more.

On top of that, Todd found himself the target of some serious female attention. They honked. They waved. They rolled down their windows and leaned out to kiss him. One stone fox even flashed him her rack. He almost fell off the median rifling his pockets for something to write down her license plate.

Just about dusk, he heard a car door open behind him and turned to see a cop climbing out of a black and white. "Show me some ID," said the cop.

"No problem," said Todd, reaching into his back pocket. Somehow, he lost his balance and stumbled toward the cop. The next thing he knew he was face down in cuffs. Within an hour, he was booked and charged with underage drinking and assaulting a police officer. "What about the anti-begging law?" he asked the DA sarcastically.

"Thanks," said the DA, adding it to the list of charges.

Todd placed an emergency collect call to his dad's law firm. "You haven't heard?" said the receptionist. "Earlier this month your father was accused of misappropriating funds. The next day he fled the country and no one's heard from him since."

"What am I supposed to do?" he said.

"I'm sure he'll find a way to get in touch with you," she said. "Good luck now!"

Todd called Zeke. He and the rest of the house agreed to put up bail. Todd lost his room for non-payment of dues, but Zeke let him sack out on the floor until the trial.

"That's it, dude," he said. "The credit window is closed."

At the trial, Todd pleaded guilty to a lesser charge and was sentenced to 60 hours of community service — at the homeless shelter. He stuffed what he could into his backpack and asked Zeke to hold the rest of his things. "Just till my dad gets in touch with me." Zeke didn't bother to answer.

Todd reported to the homeless shelter where he was put to work ladling soup. When darkness fell, he swallowed his pride and got into line with the homeless guys — just this one time. That night, the guy next to Todd smelled seriously bad. He snored, too. And sometime after midnight, someone stole Todd's belt, his best flannel shirt — and his last $20.

The next morning, he walked away from the shelter as fast as he could. He spent the day pacing slowly up and down the Mall, trying to figure out how to get in touch with his father — or any other friends or family who could help him. By late afternoon, he was ravenous. He spotted a familiar figure at a table outside Chipotle's.

"Zeke, dude," he said. "You going to finish that?"

A guy next to Zeke said, "You want me to call a cop?"

"It's okay," said Zeke. He spit on the remains of his burrito and held it out to Todd.

Dr. Julie

Dr. Julie checked her watch. Five minutes behind. She listened to her voice mail. A panicked message from Debbie, her problem client. She decided she could wait until lunch to return the call. She took a breath and went out to the waiting room to meet her new clients.

They were sitting at opposite ends of the room. He was a morose fellow of about 30, in pressed khakis and a white dress shirt. She was a pretty girl in her mid-20s, dressed in stretch jeans and a loose-fitting top — or rather she would have been pretty if not for the ferocious scowl distorting her face.

Dr. Julie introduced herself and confirmed that their names were Tom and Jill. It wasn't until Jill stood that Dr. Julie saw the reason for the stretch jeans and the loose top: This girl was five months pregnant, maybe six. Well, that certainly added a wrinkle to things.

After they'd settled onto opposite ends of her sofa and read and signed her disclosure form, Dr. Julie outlined her first session format for couple's therapy. "I'll meet with each of you separately, then we'll all talk together and discuss where we'll go from here."

Jill said she'd go first. Tom glared at her, but left without saying anything. The moment told Dr. Julie almost everything she needed to know about the dynamic between them. But identifying a client's issues was hardly ever the challenge. In contrast to that shrill radio charlatan, true therapy wasn't about hectoring people with your opinion of what they should do. It was a delicate and artful process of leading them to discover it for themselves.

"I need you to get Tom to get a job," said Jill as soon as he had left. "Ever since he lost his old one, he mopes around the house like some kind of wounded child. I was sympathetic at first, but that didn't motivate him, so I had to start pushing. It's not just for me, you know." She gestured to her swelling belly.

"So tell me about the pregnancy," said Dr. Julie. "Was it planned?"

"Not exactly, but we were eventually, you know, so it was just a matter of, you know — " In that instant, the tough veneer fell away, revealing the frightened girl beneath. Good, thought Dr. Julie. I can work with that girl.

Tom, when it was his turn, read from a written list of every occasion in the last two weeks Jill had nagged, criticized or otherwise cut him down. "You've got to get her off my back. I don't know how much more of this I can take."

Dr. Julie nodded. "So how do you feel about having a baby on the way?" she asked. Tom's face went blank and she could see the shame and confusion bubbling just beneath the surface. Okay, she thought, there's someone here to work with, too.

Dr. Julie brought Jill back in so they could all talk together. She saw that each was waiting for her to announce that it was the other who needed to change. For an instant, she let herself feel a flash of anger at both of them. Flailing away at each other and ignoring the child who was soon to be depending on them both. The anger passed as quickly as it came. She reminded herself that it was now her responsibility to help them learn to support each other as a team. And there wasn't a lot of time.

"Well," she said with a smile, "I think there are areas we can work on with both of you." Their faces fell as each considered for just an instant that they might have to change.

"Are we going to make it?" Tom blurted out, surprising himself.

"I'm quite hopeful," said Dr. Julie. "But in the end it's up to both of you."

"We have to make it," said Jill. And for a moment she and Tom turned and looked at each other. Their hands reached out across the sofa and found one another as if by reflex.

Good, thought Dr. Julie. Very good.

She concluded with some encouraging words, scheduled another session in a week and ushered the shell-shocked couple out. She glanced at her watch. Ten minutes behind. If she grabbed a quick lunch, then called Debbie, she could get herself back on schedule for the afternoon. As she grabbed her purse, she felt a wave of affection for her new clients. She hoped they made it.

She really did.

Sugar trap

Carole checked her watch. Ten after. She looked around for Chuck's Subaru. Of course it was nowhere to be found. What a fool she'd been to think divorce would change anything. He and his dysfunctions were still running her life. Stop it, Carole, she thought. Negative energy cannot be fought with more negative energy.

Making lemonade from the lemon that was her ex, Carole used the time to bring her Palm up to date and then, when Chuck still hadn't shown up, to revise the copy for her next Nexus ad. She called her agent to check on the galleys for the upcoming second edition of her breakthrough book, Escaping the Sugar Trap. Finally, she ran out of positive energy and dialed Chuck's number.

After three rings, The Martyr answered.

"Hello?"

"Vicki."

"Carole." The Martyr's voice was its usual nervous flutter. "Is Chuck there?"

"No, he's not."

"He left early to make sure he'd reach Wild Oats in time."

Carole closed her eyes. "I'm at Whole Foods. We specifically agreed to do this week's handover at Whole Foods."

"His cell's not working. I can drive to Wild Oats and

99

give him the message…"

"Chill out, Vicki. I can drive over to Wild Oats and pick up my son myself."

On the other end of the line there was that masterful little hurt silence that must work some kind of magic on Chuck but did nothing for Carole. She clicked off the phone without saying goodbye and stuffed it in her briefcase. She slammed the Range Rover into gear and charged out of the crowded lot, just missing a young couple coming out of the movie theatre. With barely contained fury she drove south on 30th to Arapahoe and then west to Broadway.

She pulled into the lot and spied the Subaru. Chuck's head was visible through the windshield, and also Jamie's little one in the back seat. As she approached the Subaru, Chuck handed something across the seat to Jamie. The sight chilled Carole's blood. It was an Oreo. She felt her whole world collapse as she watched Jamie, her only child, pull it apart and lick the creamy filling.

In three strides, Carol had reached the Subaru and yanked open the door. "What the hell do you think you're doing?" she screamed. "This is it, Chuck! This is the last straw!"

As Carole buckled Jamie into the Britax car seat, he seemed to waken from his shock and began to wail. She took out a tissue and wiped the horrid brown crumbs from his face.

On the drive home, as Jamie cried "I sowwy, Mommy" over and over in the back seat, Carole dialed Monica, her attorney. It was all so clear now. This explained everything. Jamie's speech delay. His difficulty with transitions. His sleep problems. He was a sugar junkie. And he'd been addicted by his own father.

Twenty minutes later when Carole pulled into her driveway, Monica was patiently explaining to her, "I'm sorry, Carole, but there's not a judge in America who will overturn a custody agreement just because of a cookie."

It wasn't just a cookie, of course. It was a pattern of broken promises and brazen provocations. But finally Carole had to accept that Chuck had found yet another way to torment her — with the support of an archaic judicial system.

That night Jamie was worse than usual. Whining. Restless. Bursting into tears at the slightest thing. She tried an emergency detox with red beet root, gentian and blue-green algae. If anything, Jamie's behavior got worse. He kept crying over and over to "go back to Daddy's house." Carole realized she wasn't going to win this battle by fighting fair. There was only one thing to do.

"Jamie," she said, leading him to the hall closet. "Mommy is going to give you something special. But it's a secret. You can't tell a soul. Especially Daddy."

Carole reached into the back of the top shelf and pulled out the small foil-wrapped parcel hidden there. He watched spellbound as she peeled away the foil and revealed the squares of imported Belgian chocolate. Carole broke off a piece and handed it to him. He popped it into his mouth and his eyes lit up. She felt a wave of immense guilt. How could she buy a temporary peace at the expense of her precious child's future health? She popped a piece into her own mouth and slid down to the floor. He climbed into her lap. They leaned back, each letting the creamy sweetness melt on their tongues.

"Mmm," said Jamie.

"Mmm," agreed Carole.

Yank

Lenny Gumm, Jr., DDS, patiently ground away at Mrs. Watkins' third molar. Or was it Mrs. Wilkins? He was having trouble concentrating lately. Luckily, so far, it hadn't affected his work — though he had come perilously close to pulling the wrong tooth last week. Only Diane, his trusted EDDA (Extended Duty Dental Assistant) had saved him from a momentous screw up.

"Open wide for me," he said to Mrs. W. "Open." "Wide." Those were magical words for Lenny. They were the whole reason he'd moved to Colorado. (That and the fact his father, Leonard Gumm, Sr., DDS, had caught him writing Vicodin prescriptions for his own use.) Lenny craved the sensation of freedom, of answering to no man. That's what the Vicodin had given him: precious moments of mental silence in which no inner voices were nagging him to live up to his parents' expectations.

But Colorado was better than Vicodin. For one thing, it was almost 2,000 miles from Long Island. For another, it had miles and miles of open road. Lenny's first purchase upon arriving in Boulder had been a vintage '67 Harley Davidson Electra Glide. He rode every chance he could, sometimes late into the night. It was only with the wind in his unhelmeted hair that Lenny felt at peace. Screw Zen. All he required to achieve nirvana was a Harley at full throttle. Lenny knew if he kept riding, one day he would cross over to that magic state, beyond drugs, beyond meditation, to his own perfect inner peace.

One day when he was cruising the mountains, he came upon a pack of Hell's Angels, riding two and three abreast along the narrow, windy road. On an impulse of insane proportions, Lenny accelerated himself into the middle of the pack. The bikers appeared to ignore him until, on some unseen signal, they all pulled off onto the shoulder, boxing Lenny in. It was just dawning on him he'd made a serious mistake, when he noticed the black and rotting upper incisor in the mouth of the gang's leader.

In a flash, Lenny had popped open his saddle bag and was reaching inside. The gang leader took a step toward him, his eyes clouding with suspicion. Lenny pulled out a small metal case. He snapped it open and extracted a dental scalpel.

"Open wide," he said.

Over the next three hours, Lenny did the finest work of his entire dental career. Scaling, filling, extracting. Like a missionary in a third world country, he brought balm to the throbbing mouths of the entire gang. In gratitude they presented him with a full set of leathers, and made him an honorary member with his own nickname: "Yank."

Lenny flashed back on that day as he finished seating Mrs. W's crown. "Okay," he said pulling his hands from her mouth. "You're done." He stalked out into the hallway, snapping off his gloves. "Good night," called Diane as he passed her on his way out the door.

The Harley was waiting for him in the parking lot. Its single headlight seemed to stare at him in accusation. How long had it been since Lenny had really ridden? He cruised home to his east Boulder townhouse and pulled into the garage. As the door slid down behind him, he went over to the wall and pulled down his precious leathers. He slid them on, savoring the smooth leather against his skin.

The garage door slid back up as Yank roared out into the townhouse common parking lot and off down the street. The bike was metal lightning beneath him. He rode the Diagonal up to Longmont, then cut across to Lyons and up into the mountains. Soon dusk was falling, but Yank rode on. Around each curve he hoped to spy his brothers, riding free, their hair flapping behind them like freedom flags. This time, he would stay with them, leaving "Lenny" behind forever to assume his rightful place in the world.

He circled south and then east, emerging from the mountains just north of Golden. Rocky Flats was an orangish haze as he flew past on the way to Westminster. He had Indiana to himself and he kicked it up a notch. Passing Rock Creek, he took McCaslin onto 36 and roared triumphantly back into Boulder.

Just before Colorado, a 4x4 roared through a red light and into Yank's path. With perfect reflexes, he swerved out of its way. He was home free — until a tiny oil patch broke the traction of his front tire and down the bike went. Yank's momentum carried him up and over the handlebars.

In the split second before gravity reasserted itself, Lenny reached nirvana. No voices. No doubts. No craving for the temporary high of prescription pharmaceuticals. He was once and forever free.

He didn't even mind the thought of what the impact was going to do to his dental work.

Sweet release

Jill shifted on Dr. Julie's couch. She just couldn't get comfortable. As a nurse, she had been around a lot of third-trimester women, and she knew all the physical symptoms to expect. But knowing was different than experiencing. How was she ever going to survive two and a half more months of aching back muscles, leg cramps, bad sleep, constipation — and gas? Jill had never been so gassy in her entire life. God, please don't let her embarrass herself here in front of Dr. Julie.

As a woman, you'd think Dr. Julie would show Jill some sympathy for her condition. But not today. As Jill fidgeted, Dr. Julie's questions just kept coming. "Do you think it's Tom's fault he was laid off?"

"Not exactly."

"Did he do something to cause himself to be fired? Was he irresponsible? Unreliable? Insubordinate?"

"God, no. He took more shit from Milo than I'd ever take off a boss. I mean, I used to wish he'd stand up for himself."

"So, if anything you were mad at Tom for being too concerned with keeping his job?"

"Yes, but that was before he got fired. I mean, it's a whole different situation now." Jill put a hand on her swollen belly. "I need a husband who'll do whatever it takes to find a way to bring in money for his family."

"And what has Tom been doing?"

"Well, of all things, he called Milo and asked if he

could work for him freelance."

"And?"

"Milo said sure and gave him a couple of projects."

"So, actually, Tom has found a way to bring in money."

"Yes, but it's not secure like a job. It could collapse any time."

"Just like a job could," said Dr. Julie.

"Why are you taking his side?"

"Is that what I'm doing?"

"And now you're playing that therapist game of answering a question with a question." Dr. Julie didn't respond. "You're supposed to say 'Am I?'" said Jill. No response. "It's a joke."

"Actually, I have a different question," said Dr. Julie. "Why are you so pissed off?"

Jill felt her face flush. "What kind of bullshit question is that?"

"Now you're answering a question with a question."

Jill glared at Dr. Julie, wanting to slap the calm composure off her face. "I don't know," she said. "Why do you think I'm pissed off? Or is it against the therapeutic code of conduct to actually answer a question?"

"Only for Freudians," said Dr. Julie. "I'm not surprised you want me to answer because it was, of course, a trick question. I don't, in fact, believe you are pissed off. I think that's just a big show to keep the rest of us from knowing that you're terrified."

"Terrified? Of what?"

"Facing the most overwhelming responsibility of your life with a husband who refuses to scoop you up in his strong fatherly arms and assure you everything will be all right."

Jill felt her face collapse, her eyes flood. She wailed, as months of anguish and terror poured out. "Go ahead," encouraged Dr. Julie. "You've been holding this a long time." Just then, in the midst of sobbing, Jill's body let out the longest and loudest fart of Jill's life. Jill looked at Dr. Julie in astonishment and mortification. Dr. Julie stared back, then burst out laughing. Jill started to laugh, too, like hiccups between the sobs.

Finally, she stopped. She dried her eyes with a tissue, feeling lighter than she had in months. "I guess I needed that," she said.

"Let me leave you with one final question," said Dr. Julie. "What if Tom is just as terrified as you are?"

Jill left Dr. Julie's office and walked down the stairs to the door outside. It was one of those perfect 60-degree Boulder winter days, and the sun felt like warm, tender fingers massaging her face. For a moment, Jill entertained the possibility that her life just might be okay. She might be living in one of the most beautiful places on Earth. She might be a few weeks away from bringing a precious child into the world. And Tom, the man on whom she had been blaming all her misery, just might be the soul mate she'd always wanted — if only she'd let down and give him the chance.

She wanted to race home, wrap her arms around her husband and tell him everything she had learned in her session.

Nah, she decided. Let him have his own session with Dr. Julie first.

Sweet tomato

Ray had it all. A VP slot at one of the few local high tech companies printing its annual reports in black ink. A $900,000 home in Shanahan Ridge. And a gorgeous wife and two great kids who adored him. He also had the worst case of constipation he'd ever known. His bowels were bound up tighter than those Internet pictures of that girl from "Joe Millionaire."

It all started when Ray woke up in the middle of the night with an excruciating toothache. It felt like someone was pounding a red-hot spike through his jaw. Diane drove him to the ER where a blonde and very obviously pregnant nurse took one look at him and said, "You've got an abscessed tooth."

Twenty minutes later the young and harried ER doc said the same thing, wrote out a prescription for Tylenol with codeine and told him to call his dentist in the morning. The painkillers dulled the throbbing without completely taking it away. Diane called the dental office for him the next morning, but no one answered the phone. Ray choked down some more codeine and drove himself into work. Later in the day Diane called with the news that their dentist was dead.

"They say he crashed his motorcycle," she told Ray in a stunned voice. "It took them hours to identify the remains. There wasn't even any dental work left to ID him by."

"Jesus," said Ray.

"I've been calling the other dentists on our health plan, but no one's accepting new patients."

"Keep trying," he said. "This codeine isn't doing shit for me."

Diane kept calling dentists until she found one who could see Ray the next morning. Ray made it through the night, choking down a couple of codeines every four hours. The new dentist drained the abscess, and Ray felt better almost immediately. He put away the remaining codeines and resumed his normal, busy life.

What no one had bothered to tell him was that opiates decrease peristalsis and increase stool transit time, drying out the fecal material and causing — constipation. Ray found this out the hard way a day later when he spent an hour in the morning straining to no effect. He called in sick and sent Diane to King Soopers for laxatives. She bought everything she could find, and Ray took them all: the stimulants, the stool softener, the mineral oil, the fiber cookies, even the glycerin suppositories. Then he waited for something to happen.

In the meantime, Diane had to take the kids to school. For almost an hour Ray paced the living room, feeling things shift inside him like trapped occupants in a burning building preparing but not quite ready to evacuate. He heard the mail truck out front and decided to go pick up the mail.

Ray hobbled down the driveway, fetched the mailbox's contents and hobbled back up the driveway — where he found he had locked the front door by reflex. He rattled the knob and banged on the door. Both actions only confirmed that he was alone and locked out.

Just then his colon sent the message to his brain that the laxatives had done their job and the occupants of the burning building were ready to evacuate — now! He stared around in panic. His neighbors' houses were only yards away, but there was no one he knew well enough to bang on their door and request emergency toiletry.

Ray dropped the mail on the porch and shuffled around the side of his house to the back yard. This being Shanahan Ridge, there was no privacy fence and not much of a yard. With horror, he realized he had run out of time. The occupants were going to jump — whether he was ready or not. He dove between the two cedar trees at the edge of the yard and dropped his pants.

It was over in less than a minute. Ray pulled up his pants and heaped dirt on the product of his labors. He stared around at the windows of his neighbors' houses. Had anyone seen him? He realized, this being the suburbs, he would never know.

Afterwards, he broke a window, let himself in, took a shower, dressed and drove himself to the office. Within a week he had forgotten the whole ugly business.

Six months later, Ray, taking a rare Saturday off, relaxed on the porch. Diane brought him a G&T and a BLT. He savored the drink and the sandwich. "That tomato was really tasty," he said to Diane afterwards. "Where did you get it?"

"I grow them myself," she said proudly. "In my own little garden. Right over there between the cedar trees."

Tantrum

Mila fled Belgrade seeking two things: freedom and shoes. She'd spent her childhood under communist tyranny and shoddy Romanian lace-ups, her 20s amidst the horror of the Balkan Wars and black market Kenneth Cole knockoffs, and her early 30s fleeing across Europe with whatever footwear she could jam into her backpack.

Along the way, she met and married Alan, an American touring Europe in frayed Nikes and carrying a backpack of his own. It wasn't until he brought her home to his Chautauqua mansion that she learned of his sizeable trust fund and the financial security she would be enjoying for the rest of her natural life.

Within a year she was bored to death. She had closets stuffed with every type of footwear she'd ever dreamed of and more: strappy little Anne Kleins, sexy Charles David heels, Franco Sarto boots, Bruno Magli oxfords, DKNY sandals, Doc Martens, Manolo Blahniks — she could hardly stand to look at them anymore. To her horror, she found herself actually going barefoot some days. It was as if she'd lost the very will to live.

Surprisingly, it was her husband who provided the answer. "If you hate your shoes so damn much, why don't you just sell them?"

Why not indeed? Mila decided right then and there to open her own shoe boutique. Within a week, she'd signed a lease on a storefront a block off the Mall, hired a contractor to renovate the interior and jetted over to Europe on her first buying trip. When Mila returned a month later, she drove straight from DIA to the storefront. To her dismay, the renovations were nowhere near complete. In fact, no work seemed to be going on at all. She tracked down the contractor to find out what the hell was going on.

"It's not my fault," he protested. "We hit a little snag with the city planning department over the permits." He explained he had left multiple voice mails and even spoken with a live human twice, but no one could tell him what the problem was or when it might be resolved.

"That's all you've done?" she said in disgust. "Make phone calls?" She shook her head at the utter helplessness of Americans when it came to dealing with governmental bureaucracies. Well, she hadn't grown up in a worker's paradise for nothing. It was time to take things into her own hands — or rather her feet.

The next morning, Mila dressed in her best businesswoman's suit over a divine pair of blue and white kidskin Tanino Crisci pumps. She drove to the planning department, checked her makeup in the rearview mirror, and headed inside to do battle.

"Excuse me," she said in a soft voice to the receptionist. "In one minute I will be making a scene with you. It is nothing personal and will be over soon." She then raised her voice and began to yell over and over. "I demand to see someone in authority!"

Within another two minutes a man scurried out from the back offices. "What seems to be the problem?" he said.

"Do you have authority to approve my permit?" she said.

"No, but — " Before he could say anything more,

Mila was yelling again. The man exchanged anguished glances with the secretary. "Madam, please," he said. "Don't force me to call the police."

"Call them!" shouted Mila. "Let them drag me out of here in chains! That will make a wonderful picture for tomorrow's front page!" A small crowd had gathered around Mila by now, glaring at the man. Mila took his arm. "We can continue this all day," she whispered. "Or you can take me to your supervisor and I will no longer be your problem."

The man led Mila back to an office with a sign reading "Director of Planning." He lifted his hand to knock on the door. Mila brushed past him and opened the door herself to find a woman behind a desk. Mila stepped inside and shut the door.

"Who are you?" said the woman.

"Your worst nightmare," said Mila. "A citizen who is not afraid of you."

The woman studied Mila as one dangerous animal studies another. Mila stood strong, giving no ground. Finally, the woman's eyes went to Mila's feet and visibly widened. "Where did you get those shoes?" she whispered reverently.

Mila smiled.

Twenty minutes later, she came out in her stocking feet with the approved permit in her hands. "Ah," she sighed to herself. "Bureaucracy is a fearsome beast, but it's no match for a killer pair of Italian pumps."

The question

Tom sat looking at Dr. Julie. He knew she'd asked him a question, but for the life of him he couldn't remember what it was. He thought about asking her to repeat it, but he didn't want to sound stupid. Or like he wasn't paying attention. Or like he was a total loser who couldn't even do therapy right.

"Tom?" prompted Dr. Julie.

Tom smiled at her, stalling for time. He went through the standard three questions she always asked at the beginning of a session:

"How are you?" (Okay.)

"How are things between you and Jill?" (A little better. They'd actually had a date night together without it turning into a fight.)

"How is your job search going?" (About the same. He'd landed a couple of freelance projects to supplement the unemployment, but not a single job offer.)

No, it wasn't one of the standard three. Tom remembered answering them already during this session. She must have slipped in a fourth one when he wasn't paying attention.

Could it have been a follow-up to one of the three? Probably not. He hadn't said anything to invite any kind of follow-up. Maybe that was it. Maybe she'd asked him why his answers were always so short. Why he never elaborated or volunteered any information.

Suddenly, he felt ashamed. He really was blowing this therapy stuff. He was acting like a prisoner of war under enemy interrogation. Doing his best to keep from giving away the big secret. But there was no big secret to give away. Tom may not have given Dr. Julie long, involved answers to her questions, but that didn't mean he was holding anything back.

"What more do you want from me?" he shouted silently in his head while giving nothing away on the outside. What the hell more did she want from him? He'd given her all the facts. Now, dammit, wasn't it her responsibility to start making some sense of them for him?

"Tom?" repeated Dr. Julie.

Say something. Stall for time.

"I'm thinking," he said. "It's an important question and I want to give you the right answer."

Oh great. How lame was that? Now he'd dug himself an even deeper hole. If he couldn't remember the question, not only would she know there was something wrong with his short-term memory, he'd also be revealed as a liar.

"It's not the kind of question that requires thinking," said Dr. Julie. "There's no right or wrong answer."

Shit. Wait, that was a clue. No thinking. No right or wrong answer. If he could just take a guess.

"Tom?" she said again.

Oh hell. There was no way he was going to remember. Time to give it up.

"I'm sorry," Tom said softly. "What was the question?"

"How are you feeling?"

Of course! God, how could he have forgotten something so simple? How was he feeling? How was he feeling? He could answer this one.

"Fine," he said. Good, now they could move on. They could talk about Jill's behavior and getting her to lighten up on — .

"Let me rephrase the question," said Dr. Julie. "What emotion are you feeling?"

Tom looked at Dr. Julie. Suddenly he realized she'd asked him another question and he'd spaced it out again. Shit, shit, shit. He looked down at his feet.

"Tom?" prompted Dr. Julie.

He looked up at her. She patiently waited for him to say something. He racked his brain, trying to figure out what she'd asked.

"I'm fine," he said again, hoping it was the right answer.

"Bullshit," said Dr. Julie. Tom stared at Dr. Julie. She smiled at him and repeated softly, "Bullshit."

Tom was speechless. He felt his face flush red.

"Let's try this again," she said. "You're out of work. You're collecting unemployment insurance while you call up employers and beg them to give you a job. Meanwhile, you're less than two months away from being a father and you don't have a clue how you're going to cope. So, to repeat the question: How do you feel?"

"How do I feel?" Tom blurted out. "How do you think I feel?" The words poured out of him like lava from an erupting volcano. "I'm pissed off and confused and terrified out of my mind!" he shouted at her.

"Ah," said Dr. Julie with a smile. "Now we're getting somewhere."

Cookie

Cassie was laid off in July. She cut her budget to the bone. She clipped coupons, bought generic and scoured the grocery aisles for Sooper Card specials. She broke down and took in a roommate who gave her $450 toward the rent and utilities. Even with all that, she still found her credit card balances creeping up.

Some days she was able to channel her constant panic into making job calls and sending out resumes. Other days it was all she could do to sit in her bathrobe and watch Oxygen for hours on end.

Just when she thought things couldn't get any harder, one snowy Saturday in February she made a trip to the store and spied the card table set up in the entranceway.

"Oh God," she said to herself. "Please let it be anything but — " Then she spied the young girls in their uniforms, the little rectangular boxes in their delicate hands. Cassie froze in her tracks, wringing her hands in helplessness. It was the last straw. It was the end of the world. It was the one ordeal she had not counted on...

Girl Scout Cookie time.

More persistent than a pledge drive, more guilt inspiring than a "save the baby seals" direct mail campaign, there was no way Cassie's battered self-esteem and/or anemic budget could survive the assault that lay ahead. She turned around, slunk back to her Mazda and drove home.

For almost a week, she managed with supplies on hand, but finally she couldn't face one more macaroni and cheese dinner. She needed fresh food. She had to go to the store. She waited until 9:00, figuring the girls would be home in bed.

Wrong.

They surrounded Cassie the instant she set foot in the store. "Would you like to buy some Girl Scout cookies?"

Cassie mumbled "No, thanks," and pushed her way past. She stumbled through the store, feeling like the lowest person in the world. She couldn't purge her mind's eye of those cute little faces looking up at her. And she hadn't even had the guts to tell them the truth: "Sorry, sweet little girl scout, but I'm so broke I can't afford to buy your over-priced and fat-laden cookies."

But was it really the truth? Couldn't she do without, say, two cans of tuna and use the money for cookies? But tuna would feed her for days and she didn't even really like cookies. And when did the Girl Scouts stop going door to door and start setting ambushes in grocery store lobbies? What kind of lesson was that teaching them?

By the time Cassie was finished shopping, she had worked herself up into a state of outrage. This time as she headed out the door, she stared down the little parasites, cowing them with the force of her glare.

She felt proud of herself for about 20 seconds. Then she felt like the biggest heel in the universe. She berated herself all the way home, then into the apartment and even in bed with the lights out. The next morning, after a sleepless night, she realized she had forgotten to buy laundry detergent. She considered using dishwashing detergent or even shampoo.

"Get a grip, Cassie," she told herself. "Be a grown-up."

She got back in the Mazda and drove for the store. At the last minute, she drove past, telling herself there was more than one grocery store in Boulder. Over the next four hours, she drove to store after store after store. At every one, she parked her car, walked hopefully toward the door and turned around when she saw yet another card table stacked high with Samoas, Thin Mints, Trefoils, Tagalongs, DoSiDos, Ole Oles and All Abouts.

Finally, she sat in her car in a parking lot in Longmont. Her trip odometer showed almost 300 miles. Her emotional resources were shot. She could hold out no longer. She wiped her face with a leftover Taco Bell-recycled brown paper napkin, finger-brushed her hair and went inside.

"Would you like to buy some — ?"

Cassie shoved a $10 bill into the nearest little hand and walked into the store. She went to the laundry aisle and found a 7.12-pound box of generic detergent on sale for half-price. Maybe this was the universe's way of telling her she had done the right thing.

Cassie paid for the detergent, smiled at the cashier and took her change. She headed out for the parking lot through a different door than she had come in by. She smiled at the inevitable card table — until she realized with horror that instead of cookies, the table was covered with Muscular Dystrophy shamrocks.

Murder Town

Kevin's proudest moment came when he was kicked out of drama school. Not for his unauthorized all-nude production of *You're A Good Man, Charlie Brown*. Not for his 13-word essay on Aristophanes: "He was the Neil Simon of his time. I refuse to discuss him." No, the breaking point was when he took his "Realism in Acting" class hostage, held a gun to the teacher's head and gave her a nervous breakdown. She threatened to file charges, but he knew it was just professional jealousy.

He left school happily, certain they had nothing to teach him. They were moral cowards like everyone else. Afraid to look into the abyss. Kevin had nothing but scorn for them and everyone else who would rather watch *The Sound of Music* (his own favorite musical up until the age of 12) than face the darkness at the heart of human existence.

Kevin moved to Boulder to plan his next move. Before long, he had attracted a loyal following of actors who admired his unflinching vision. "We need to shock the audience out of their complacency," he said one night in Penny Lane. "I have just the idea." He paused dramatically. *Murder Town: The Musical*. Singing and dancing reenactments of Boulder's most notorious murders. It's black humor, it's camp, it's Grand Guinol, it's — "

"Cool," his followers said in unison.

The first step was to decide on the murders. "There's that Chase girl," said Kevin. "And that hit-and-run by the stripper speeding on Broadway."

"How about the girl who got stabbed in that store by that deranged butcher knife killer?" said Clarissa.

"Perfect," said Kevin.

"We have to do JonBenet, of course," added Doug.

Kevin gave him a withering glance. "Of course," he said. "That's our grand finale."

One sleepless, caffeinated week later, they had a script. It was over-the-top-edgy brilliant. From the opening number featuring the dance sequence from *Singing in the Rain* (substituting a butcher knife for Gene Kelly's umbrella) to the finale starring Kevin in a *Cats* costume singing "Memory" while strangling a life-size doll. A week later they had arranged to rent two off-nights at the Dairy. The next four weeks were spent in rehearsals, stapling up posters and strong-arming friends into agreeing to come.

Two nights before opening, Kevin got home at three in the morning. He opened his apartment door and before he had time to react, his dog Artaud scooted through his legs and out onto the street. The Grand Cherokee didn't even stop, flinging Artaud 20 feet onto the sidewalk. Kevin ran to him, cradled his shuddering body and felt the life go out of him.

At that moment, Kevin felt himself go numb. He watched himself driving Artaud's body to the 24-hour vet clinic to arrange for cremation. He had no interest in sleep or food. He sleepwalked through the final dress rehearsal. He could see the others watching him, but none of them dared say anything to his face.

Opening night he forced himself to push aside his numbness for a few minutes. He gathered the cast and gave the inspirational speech of his life. "Murder is the perfect metaphor for our art. We must kill the complacency of our audience. We must slaughter convention. We must slash people to their core and force them to stop numbing themselves with martinis, Prozac and Andrew Lloyd Weber." He held them rapt, reducing his voice to a whisper. "Now let's go out there — and kill."

The audience was small but enthusiastic. They laughed at the opening number and applauded loudly. It quickly turned into one of those magic nights in theatre when a cast and audience are perfectly in tune. The audience inspired the actors to reach higher, which brought more response, which drove the actors even more.

The night went by in a blur for Kevin. Soon it was time for his big moment, the finale. He zipped up his cat suit and took the doll from Clarissa. "Knock 'em dead," she whispered, kissing his cheek.

He stepped onto the stage and suddenly his numbness fell away. The music began, but he couldn't open his mouth to sing. He stared into the lights and it was like looking into an abyss. Not the tiny crevasse he had always taken for an abyss. But an impossibly deep darkness yawning beneath him. A darkness in which death was real and final and cruel and arbitrary.

The audience gaped at him as tears poured down his face. The doll in his arms felt like a lifeless dog and also a 6-year-old girl choked to death in a basement room.

The music played on. The cat suit hung heavy like a shroud. And all Kevin wanted was to be 12 and watching *The Sound of Music*.

Visions of war

It was a weird day. By afternoon, the snow had finally stopped. People layered on their sweat shirts, parkas and boots, and started digging out. There was almost a festive air. Shovelers chatted with the virtual strangers who were their neighbors. People made snowmen, snow forts, sled jumps. For a few precious hours everyone forgot the dread hanging over the country — and the world.

That night, safely back in their private places they, one-by-one, got the news.

Dorothy had NPR on low while she was mending an old, comfy sweater. In mid-darn, she recognized Bush's unmistakable drone. She turned up the radio. Less than a minute later she turned it off. She sat completely still. Her mind filled with images of dead and mutilated children and dead and mutilated soldiers who were after all only kids themselves. All at the whim of one petulant child pretending to be a world leader. She cried tears of grief for the anguish to come, of rage at her own powerlessness in the face of evil, and of shame for her country.

Jake was driving his 4x4 pickup to Aces to replenish his cache of beer when he heard the President. Jake wanted to shout with joy and pound the horn. Instead he allowed himself some quiet exhilaration. The UN was finished. The US had once and for all shown the mongrel world that the White Christian nation could and would do whatever it damn well wanted to. And the Bill of Rights was being rewritten to no longer apply to dark-skinned men with foreign accents. The rumor that had been circulating through the Militia underground was true: they really did have one of their own in the White House.

Crystal felt the harmonic disturbance in the middle of her evening meditation. (At least that's how she would remember it. Actually, her best friend Lissa had called her with the news.) Crystal immediately lit every candle in her studio apartment, saged and sweetgrassed everywhere and put on a Carlos Nakai CD. She chanted and prayed to Universal Consciousness to change its path of conflict to a path of peace. When the CD was done she stood, stretched and blew out the candles. Only time would tell if her work would have an effect. In the meantime, she made a note to schedule a massage for the next day. In times of global imbalance, it was important to pamper yourself.

Jack was surfing Persian Kitty on the home office computer when his oldest son Reed burst in. "The war just started!" he said as Jack quickly navigated to MSNBC.com. Yes, there it was. "Breaking News." He shook his head solemnly and gave Reed a look of deep seriousness. Inside he was going "Yes!" The boil had finally been lanced. The uncertainty was over. Now the markets would rebound. The economy would perk up. Housing prices would rise. Soon, he could stop worrying about maxing out the HELOC. Commission checks would start coming again. Things were going to be okay after all. He tousled Reed's hair and said a silent prayer of gratitude it wasn't his kids on the front line.

Tom was lying on a hot pad to soothe his aching lower back. Jill fussed over him and kept her judgements to herself by not saying, "That's what you get for trying to overcompensate for your feelings of financial inadequacy by shoveling the entire driveway and sidewalk and half the street." She settled her extremely pregnant body into the recliner and picked up the remote control.

"You mind if I check the news?" she said.

Tom grunted. She decided that meant okay and clicked the remote. Instead of Larry King, there was the President announcing that the war had started. She grabbed her belly as if to protect her baby from the horrible news. What kind of world was this they were bringing him or her into? Would the next twenty years be filled with wars and terrorism and dying? Would their child some day be blown up in front of their eyes?

On the couch, Tom grunted, "Good. Maybe now at least things can start to get back to normal."

Jill threw the remote at his head, raising a nasty bruise.

In the foothills, Lea was asleep, dreaming of the day's hunt. She had trapped a doe in a narrow ravine, jumped it, and broke its neck cleanly with a shake of her jaws. She ate leisurely, purring loudly at the pleasure of a slowly filling belly. When she was sated, she buried the leftovers beneath a tree and climbed a nearby rock to sleep. Somewhere nearby, a hundred thousand TVs announced news of earth-shattering importance to the humans sitting in front of them.

It didn't disturb Lea's sleep a bit.

Dr. Julie loses it

Dr. Julie woke with a monster headache. She'd only managed a few hours of sleep. Mostly because of the late-night "discussion" with her husband David. He'd started it by saying something to the effect that since the war had started, they should mute their protest to support the troops. Dr. Julie replied that the real way to support them was to force Bush to bring them home. He told her she was narcissistically assuming the whole world revolved around her actions. She accused him of overcompensating for his own feelings of male inadequacy. God, was there anything more pathetic than two therapists fighting?

Now, she had to get up and spend her day counseling other people on their relationships. She showered, choked down some strong coffee and threw on the only clean work outfit in her closet. The first couple of the morning were Jill and Tom. She was quite proud of the work she had done with them. She had used cognitive therapy to get Tom to recognize and challenge the negative internal voices that kept him emotionally shut down. She had helped Julie confront the childhood roots of her controlling and criticizing behavior. They had turned out to be exceptional clients, making major progress in a very short time. And none too soon. Jill's maternity blouse looked like a tablecloth stretched over a beach ball.

Dr. Julie began the session with the usual "How are

you doing?" She was pleased to note that Tom was able to name his feelings in his check-in while Jill spoke about herself without blaming Tom for her situation. She acknowledged them both and watched as they basked in her praise.

Her plan for the day's session was to build on their individual growth by challenging them to apply what they'd each learned about themselves to their marriage. But first she decided to give them a quick and simple relationship building exercise. "I want you to face one another and each tell the other one thing you appreciate about them."

Tom and Jill turned toward one another. Tom smiled nervously. Jill cleared her throat. They turned to Dr. Julie. For heaven's sake, she thought.

"Jill, why don't you go first?"

"Okay," said Jill. "Well, I guess I appreciate that Tom is getting off his butt and finding work — even if it is only freelance and even if he sat around for months and even if — "

"Jill!" Dr. Julie interrupted. She felt the morning's headache return like a vise. "Can you start again and this time focus on the positive without any negativity creeping in?"

"You're right," said Jill. "I'm sorry. I really am glad that Tom is getting work."

"Thank you," said Dr. Julie. "Tom?" He sat looking at his lap. "Tom?"

"I guess I'm still hearing the things Jill said before. And when she talks like that, I don't appreciate anything about her."

The vise around Dr. Julie's head tightened.

"I said I was sorry."

"I don't believe you."

"Screw you."

Tom turned to Dr. Julie with his best "poor little me" expression on his face.

"What the hell is the matter with you two?!" Dr. Julie heard herself shout. "You're two grown-up, intelligent people who love each other! For God's sake, why can't you just be kind to each other?!"

Dr. Julie slumped back in her chair. Tom and Jill stared at her open-mouthed. Oh, shit, she thought. What the hell did I just do? "I'm sorry," she said. "That was inexcusable of me."

"No," said Tom. "You're right. We're like two children throwing tantrums at each other."

"It's so stupid," agreed Jill, taking Tom's hand. "Why can't we stop attacking each other long enough to remember that we need each other?"

He reached for her and they both hugged, tears coming to their eyes.

Dr. Julie felt tears come to her own eyes. Not for the first time, she felt humbled by her own clients and the way they could take her flawed efforts and use them for their own growth. She resolved to herself to go home that night, wrap her arms around David and just love him.

For as long as he kept his mouth shut about the war.

One-on-one

D r. Maxwell was a serious man. His bearing was formal, his diction precise, his grammar impeccable. The only vanity he allowed himself was the framed Ph.D. on his office wall. He was the first in his family to finish high school, the first to attend college and the first to receive a graduate degree. The first to rise so far above the mass of whites who had taken his inferiority for granted.

He was now welcomed, at least superficially, into the majority culture. He served on the boards of major corporations and had shaken the hands of three presidents. In his spare time, he spoke to African-American youth groups, seeking to inspire them. Most importantly, he sought to open their horizons beyond sports and rap music.

"You are the noble descendents of a proud people," he would say. "You can be more than performing animals or clowns. You must respect yourself and live a life that demands respect from others."

With his single-minded focus, he didn't marry until late. And long after he had given up on fatherhood, his son was born. His wife, Alice, insisted on an African name. They settled on Bakari (Swahili for "One who will succeed") Robert Maxwell.

The proud father made sure the nursery was filled with books and art. He placed a CD player beside the crib and played Mozart and Miles Davis as his son slept. When the baby was awake, Dr. Maxwell spoke to him of his heritage and of the responsibility he carried to make something great of his life.

Soon Bakari was a loud and active toddler. All he wanted to do was climb and jump and hang upside down from his father's arms. Dr. Maxwell told his son to sit still and listen to him. Bakari wriggled away and ran laughing to jump on his bed. Dr. Maxwell was storming after him when Alice pulled him aside.

"He's a little boy," she said. "He needs you to love and accept him as he is."

Dr. Maxwell compromised. He still read educational books to Bakari and spoke to him of his heritage and responsibility. But he also rolled up his $200 Egyptian-cotton sleeves and did his middle-aged best to play with his son.

Soon Bakari started school. He was a bright child and did well at the subjects that interested him, such as reading and music and especially phys. ed. Dr. Maxwell's eyes widened with anger at the Cs in math, science and history. He told Bakari he was grounded until he brought his grades up.

Again Alice stepped in to warn her husband that his efforts to win the battle of academics might very well lose him the war for his son's heart. So again, Dr. Maxwell compromised. He mounted a basketball hoop on the garage and let Bakari play with his friends for an hour after school. In return, every night, Bakari accepted his father's help with homework in math, science and history.

Dr. Maxwell bided his time, certain his son would eventually outgrow childish games. Instead when seventh grade arrived, Bakari went out for the school basketball team and won a spot. This infuriated Dr. Maxwell, but his son continued to do his homework every night, so he reserved judgement.

The night of the first game, they rode to the school gym in silence. Inside, Dr. Maxwell insisted on sitting in the back row. He felt his face redden as the loudspeakers blared hip hop and the young cheerleaders pranced like hussies. He also was very conscious of all the white faces in the stands — and on the court. Bakari was the only black player on either team. He was also the best player by far. From the opening whistle, he dominated the game with his speed and athleticism.

For the entire time, Dr. Maxwell sat with folded arms and a scowl. Afterwards, he was the first out the door, heading into the shadows behind the gym building to calm himself and prepare something appropriate to say to his son. Beside him, light spilled through a open window. Along with the light came the raucous sounds of a winning locker room. One of the voices said, "Hey, Bakari, wanna stay after and play some one-on-one?"

"No thanks," came Bakari's voice. "I'm riding home with my old man."

"Yeah, right. Mr. 'If-I-Dress-and-Talk-All-Fancy-No-One-Will-Notice-I'm-a-Negro.'"

The entire locker room went silent. Dr. Maxwell felt his face flush, his breath catching in his chest. After what seemed like an eternity, Bakari spoke in a soft but firm voice. "My father is the noble descendent of a proud people and he is the best man I've ever known. If you or anyone else in this room ever disses him again, I'm off the team."

In the darkness, Dr. Maxwell's breath filled his chest as his heart soared and his face burned with pride. Without conscious intent, his hands hoisted an imaginary ball and launched it into the darkness. It flew in a perfect arc toward a precious goal that for the moment somehow seemed not quite so distant or unreachable.

Inner millionaire

"Manifest your prosperity," Crystal counseled Danny. They were riding side-by-side on the Boulder Creek bike trail. He squirted some Glycomax into his mouth and considered her advice.

"How do I do that?" he asked.

"Starting today, live like you have a million dollars in the bank."

Actually, Danny did have a million dollars in the bank. A million three to be exact. The problem, of course, was the trust—or rather the trustee, a stuffy lawyer Grandmother had put in place before she died. George, like Grandmother, was financially conservative. And he doled out Danny's "allowance" accordingly.

Well, screw him! Whose money was it anyway? Who had spent literally months of his childhood visiting Grandmother in the hospice? Who had smelled the stink of her cancer? Who kissed her cadaverous cheeks? By God, Danny had earned that money. And Crystal was right. It was time he started living like the millionaire he was.

Crystal split for her afternoon healing circle. Danny rode a while longer, considering just what it was millionaires did with their money. Well, some made big political contributions, but that was a bore. Some bought mansions in Vail they visited twice a year, but Danny was pretty sure that took more than a million three. Some hired lots of servants, but Danny didn't want that kind of karmic debt on his soul.

Finally he hit on the perfect thing: a luxury car! No, bigger than that: an SUV!

Danny didn't even bother going by his apartment. He rode straight to the nearest car dealer. Striding boldly inside, he walked up to the biggest, most option-laden, four-wheel-drive behemoth in the showroom and said, "I'll take it."

The salesman nearly wet himself as he watched Danny write out a check for the entire list price plus tax and license. The sales manager insisted on calling Danny's bank, but Danny gave him the number for the trust account and the moment the sales manager heard the balance, he handed Danny the keys.

Thirty minutes later Danny was cruising. He stroked the all-leather interior and turned up the satellite radio. He looked down on the smaller cars below him and felt richer already. He glanced ahead. There was a lane closure coming up. He jerked the wheel left, cutting off a Subaru. Horns honked and an angry finger was extended his way. He found it didn't bother him at all.

He dialed the hands-free cell phone. "Crystal, it's Danny," he said into her answering machine. "You'll never guess what I'm doing. Call me." He laughed to himself, slapping the steering wheel with glee.

Danny accelerated, relishing the feel of gas-guzzling American power at his fingertips. He knew all of his friends considered SUVs to be environmentally disastrous. More than one of them called SUV drivers "supporters of terrorism" because Saudi oil money bankrolled Osama bin Laden.

Well, screw them! Boulder was still a part of America, and in America it was no crime to be rich and spend money. Danny closed his eyes for a second to imagine the looks on his friends' faces when he pulled up in front of their houses. He closed his eyes for literally one second.

It was long enough for the SUV to rear-end another car with a sickening crash. Danny's eyes flew open. In front of him was a crumpled hatchback. Old and rusty and driven by a Mexican-looking lady with three kids in the back. He closed his eyes and laid his head down on the steering wheel. He thought about driving off or getting out to help or calling the police.

Instead, he called George.

A few hours later, Danny was riding in George's BMW while George's condescending voice informed him he was lucky the woman had accepted a cash settlement in lieu of pressing charges, and luckier still George had been able to talk the dealer into taking back the SUV "at a significant loss." Still, Danny had demonstrated an appalling lack of restraint, and George would be cutting back on his allowance accordingly.

Danny slumped in his seat, eyes closed, doing his best to tune out the lecture. Yes, he had made an error in judgement and things had not worked out exactly well. But George was wrong. The problem was not Danny's lack of restraint. If anything, Danny hadn't been bold enough. The gods punish those who settle for too little. No, Danny would not make the same mistake twice. No ordinary SUV for this millionaire.

Next time he would get a Hummer.

Last ride

Tom glanced at Jill asleep on the couch. She had-n't been able to find a comfortable position last night and thus hadn't slept a wink. Not to mention getting up every half hour to pee. The ninth month of pregnancy was hell. Of course, it wasn't a picnic for him either. Her tossing and sighing and getting in and out of bed hadn't exactly made it easy for Tom to sleep a wink himself.

But now she was out cold, and Tom saw his own opportunity to get out. He eased open the door from the kitchen into the garage, slipped through, and ever so gently pulled it closed. He stood for a moment, wait-ing for Jill's voice to call out his name.

Nothing.

He scooped up his helmet, lowered his Pinarello from its rack and walked it down the driveway. He continued down the block before stopping to inflate the soggy tires with his hand pump. Every second, he expected to hear Jill's voice yelling for him to come back and fetch something for her or rub her ankles or listen to her bitch about varicose veins and hemorrhoids.

Once inflation was complete, Tom mounted the bike, slipped his feet into the clips and rode along Moorhead to the bike path. He coasted down the incline and once on the path, accelerated. He took it easy at first, letting his body settle into the bike.

It had been months since he'd last ridden. Mostly because of the weather, but also because he'd been in emotional survival mode due to the pregnancy and being laid off and almost losing his marriage.

After two months of couple's therapy, Tom no longer worried about losing his marriage. Now he only worried about losing his freedom, his balanced life, his mind and his God-given right to ride his bicycle on a sunny Saturday afternoon.

The sun felt good on his skin. Like a lover's caress. Even better. The sun didn't expect any small talk or flowers or midnight trips to the kitchen to make peanut butter and pickle sandwiches. Tom tried to shrug off thoughts of Jill and let himself melt into the ride. Muscle memory kicked in, and he felt that old feeling of utter peace in motion.

He came to a fork in the path and realized he could turn around and probably make it back home in time to be there when Jill awoke from her nap. Instead Tom blew past. He wended his way north, heading for the Diagonal.

With every cycle of the pedals, he felt calmer, more self-possessed, more centered. The anxieties he had been living with, as well as ones so horrible he had been repressing them, no longer seemed to have any power over him. He could look at them dispassionately, seeing them like harmless images projected on his mental Cineplex.

He saw Jill dying in childbirth. He saw their child coming out with an unspeakable birth defect. He saw their child being born in perfect health but finding he felt no love for it.

The images began to come faster. Tom saw himself selling his bike to pay for a backyard play set or a baby jogger. He saw himself pushing that jogger while wearing a backpack full of bottles, diapers, baby wipes and pacifiers.

He saw himself losing contact with all his childless friends. He saw himself becoming a bore with snap-shots and stories of sleepless nights, first smiles, first words. He saw himself lying down at night too tired for sex. He saw himself worrying over bills and account balances and college funds.

He saw himself rushing his child to the Emergency Room with a high fever. He saw himself rushing his child to the Emergency Room with a concussion. He saw himself saying stupid things like "You'll put your eye out," "Because I said so," and "I'll give you some-thing to cry about."

He saw himself holding his child in his arms for the first time, staring down into the face of that tiny stranger, and knowing he would do everything in his power to protect it, including laying down his own life if necessary.

He saw himself becoming a father.

The sun was over the Flatirons by now, and Tom was nearing Longmont. His legs ached. His ass throbbed from the hard seat. He knew it was way past time for him to turn around and head home. Instead he kept going. He knew he wouldn't keep riding forever. He would turn around eventually and retrace his path and give himself back up to the extraordinary life that awaited him.

Just not quite yet.

Saturday

Quentin woke up. He was alone. Excitedly, he squirmed free of the tangled bedclothes. He ran out and down to the door at the end of the hall. Twisting the knob with both hands, he pushed the door open.

He tiptoed to the bed. The two figures under the sheets were asleep. He carefully took a giant step back, whispered "ready, set, go," and launched himself up and onto the bed.

Mommy shrieked. Daddy yelled, "What the hell?!"

Quentin giggled and wormed his way up to the head of the bed between them. "Good morning," he said, flashing his most innocent smile.

Daddy tried to grumble, but Quentin could tell that he didn't really mean it. Quentin jumped up and down on the bed, shouting "I want pancakes!"

In the kitchen Mommy mixed the batter while Quentin dragged his purple plastic step stool over to the counter. "I want to stir!" he said, grabbing for the spoon. Mommy handed it to him, and he stirred and stirred until his arm ached. Some of the batter slopped out onto the counter — and onto Quentin.

"Look at the mess you've made!" said Mommy. Quentin dropped the spoon. His eyes burned. His throat and chest felt tight.

"It's no big deal, little man," said Daddy, placing a strong hand on Quentin's back. "We'll clean it up

140

together."

After breakfast, Quentin put on jeans and his favorite Bob the Builder T-shirt. He played out back with his dump truck. Under a bush he found a dead bird. He looked up at the house. Mommy and Daddy were reading the paper on the deck. Quentin knew he wasn't supposed to touch dead things. He tried really hard not to. But his hand reached out anyway.

A thunderous "Quentin Alexander!" came from the deck. Quentin dropped the bird. He stood up to run, but Daddy picked him up and carried him inside, kicking and screaming, to the Time Out chair.

Quentin was playing "Little Monster at School" when Mommy said, "Time to turn off the computer and get ready to go to Grandmother's."

"No!" moaned Quentin. Mommy turned off the computer and led him out to the car. He kicked the back of Daddy's seat until Daddy said, "Don't make me stop this car!"

Grandmother's house smelled funny. So did Grandmother. She pulled Quentin to her birdlike face and kissed him. He squirmed away. The only toys she had were some yucky blocks from when Daddy was a little boy. Lunch was yucky, too. Afterwards, Quentin pulled Grandmother's cat's tail until it yowled and scratched his arm. Quentin cried. They went home.

Later Mommy made a bath for Quentin. Some of his favorite bath toys were missing. He tried to climb out of the tub to look for them, but Mommy said, "Get back in there." Quentin sulked until the bath was over. When Mommy tried to dry him with a towel, he whined, "No, I'm a big boy." Mommy let him dry himself. When he was done she handed him the green pajamas.

"I want the purple pajamas," he said.

"They're in the wash," said Mommy.

"I hate you," said Quentin.

Mommy forced the green pajamas on the miserable Quentin, then carried him into his room. "Pick one story for Daddy to read you," she said.

"I want two."

"You get one."

Quentin slouched over to the bookshelves and thumbed through the books.

"I want 'Horton Hears a Hoot.'"

"It's 'Horton Hears a Who,'" said Mommy, "and we took it back to the library yesterday. Pick another one."

"I don't want another one!"

"Okay if you don't want a book tonight that's your choice."

Quentin glared at her, his lip quivering. He grabbed "Where the Wild Things Are" and dragged it to the bed. Daddy came in and read to him. Quentin said almost all the words along with Daddy from memory.

When Daddy was done, he tucked Quentin in. Mommy handed him his bear. They hugged him one last time and went out, shutting the door behind him. Quentin lay completely still, listening for monsters. He heard a noise and cried out, "Help, help!"

Daddy opened the door, said, "Go to sleep," and shut the door again.

Quentin sniffled and whispered, "I hate you."

When his parents looked in on him on the way to bed, they found him fast asleep, storing up enough energy to get him through his next day. They stood for a while, taking in his peaceful, angelic face, storing up enough love to get them through theirs.

Neighbor Moment

Big Al had more body hair than the average Boulderite, but that wasn't saying much. People bitched about Texans and Californians invading the place, but everyone Big Al met seemed to be from Minnesota. Each specimen pinker and more hairless than the last.

He'd only left Brooklyn for Boulder to deal with his mother's estate — in particular the fully-paid-for bi-level she'd left him. His plan was to slap it on the market, pocket the windfall and escape back home.

Somehow six months later he was still here. He'd changed realtors twice, but none of them had been able to get him an offer anywhere close to his asking price. So he hung out in the house. It wasn't costing him anything, after all. And he tried his best to get along with the natives. But it wasn't easy.

"Every time I try to talk to one of my neighbors," he said to Andy, another former Brooklynite and Big Al's only real friend in Boulder, "they hurry off, give me the cold shoulder or look at me like I'm some kind of freak."

"You are," said Andy. "Never forget this is a totally foreign culture with its own special customs."

"What do you mean?"

"First off, you can't just walk up to someone and start talking."

"Why not?"

143

"They'll think you're a psycho. You have to create what I call the Neighbor Moment."

"Neighbor Moment?"

"There are several varieties, but let's start with the most basic: the Mailbox Moment. It's morning. You walk down the driveway to check the mail. Your neighbor is checking his mail, too. You smile. If he smiles, you nod. If he nods, you say something like, 'Can you believe all this junk mail?' He'll say something like, 'I know what you mean.' You say, 'Have a good one,' and go back inside. Mailbox Moment complete."

"But I didn't even get a chance to say anything."

"Exactly the point. He feels safe. He begins to trust you to keep your distance and never ask anything of him that he'll either have to give in and do or feel uncomfortable saying no."

Big Al shook his head. "So then what?"

"Then you can move on to a Yard Moment," Andy patiently explained. "You start off by doing something in your front yard. Weeding, watering, digging, it doesn't matter. Just be out there doing some kind of chore."

"Then what?"

"You wait. It may not happen the first day. Or the second. But sooner or later the neighbor will be working in his yard, too. Or taking out the garbage. Or going for a walk with the wife. The point is to be concentrating on your work so he can come over and say, 'Working hard?'"

"Now can I talk to him?"

"Only to say, 'Not really.' Then if you've played it right, he'll say something like, 'We sure could use some rain,' or 'I need to prune the junipers, but I'm putting it off as long as I can.' Who knows? He might even go so far as to introduce himself. And the wife if she's there. They might even welcome you to the neighborhood."

"Now we're getting somewhere."

"Which is why you say, 'Well I better get back to my digging,' and let them head off for their stroll. Then if you've played things right, you'll move on to the Barbecue Moment."

"I invite them over?"

"They invite you over. They'll say, 'Don't bring anything.' So you bring some imported beer or homemade potato salad with new potatoes and dill. She'll offer you a margarita. You say, 'Sounds good.' He'll say, 'How about refreshing mine while you're at it, hon.' She'll say, 'Isn't this your third?' He'll give her a look and say, 'Who's counting?' Then while she's in the kitchen pouring, he'll start some small talk that will rapidly devolve into spilling his guts about his ex, his step-kids, his asshole of a boss, his chronic prostatitis and his complete lack of a sex life. Then as soon as dinner's over, you'll make some excuse to go home early. And for the next six months, you'll look out the window before you step outside, avoid working in the yard and only check the mailbox after dark — anything to keep the poor loser from cornering you into an I-Don't-Have-Any-Friends-But-Would-You-Be-My-Friend? Moment."

It was after midnight when Big Al got home and into bed. He woke up and chuckled to himself, remembering Andy's ridiculous story. He slipped on his robe and headed out the door to pick up the mail. The guy next door just happened to be getting his mail, too. The neighbor smiled and gave Big Al a nod.

"Can you believe all this junk mail?"

April shower

It was finally here. The day Jill had been dreading from the moment the pregnancy test showed positive. The day other women had warned her about. The day whose sheer anguish no man would ever truly understand.

Her baby shower.

She'd tried her best not to have one. She'd pled work pressure. She'd insisted there was nothing she needed. She'd thrown herself on the mercy of her closest friends, begging them to spare her the indignity.

In the end it was Tom's mother June (in town for a two-week visit) who'd caught her in a moment of weakness. "It's not just for you, dear. It's an intimate moment to share with all the women in your life who love you and want to celebrate your happiness." June patted Jill's knee. "And I promise nothing will happen to embarrass you or make you uncomfortable."

Jill said yes, wanting to believe her mother-in-law's promise. And she did manage to keep believing it — right up to the moment she walked inside her best friend Carol's house. The walls were covered with blow-ups of Jill's most embarrassing baby pictures: the one where she was wearing nothing but a cowgirl hat, the one where she was reading a picture book on the potty and, of course, the one taken at the moment of her birth — red, puffy, fists clenched and screaming at the top of her tiny lungs.

The party plates featured cartoon diapered piglets with squealing faces. The punch was served in baby bottles (complete with nipples). At the door each guest was given three clothespins to fasten to her blouse with the instruction that every time she said the word "baby" she'd have to give a pin to the mother-to-be. At the end of the party, the one with the most pins remaining would win a prize.

Jill took a seat on the sofa, staring around at all the guests. She could have sworn she didn't know half of them. So much for her "intimate moment."

Before she knew it the games began. Jill sent up a desperate prayer they would be dignified and restrained. She might as well have hoped for a US president with a three-digit IQ.

The first game was the tamest. Paper plates with little dabs of baby food were passed around. The guests had to taste the samples and guess what each one was. People laughed, some gagged at the sweet potatoes, squash or peas. But all in all, if this was the worst, Jill could live with it.

The next game was a modified version of Twister in which everyone but Jill was required to wear a 20-pound weight belt. Jill tried to stay on the couch but was dragged out onto the floor anyway. Her hemorrhoids were on fire and her lower back screamed, what the hell are you doing to me? So Jill fell on purpose early in the game, accidentally landing on Amy's ankle. Jill volunteered to drive her to the ER, but Amy just laughed and said, "Nice try."

The final game was the worst and most tasteless. Everyone was led to the dining room table and offered a plate with a folded diaper resting in the middle. Carol shouted "Go!" and they all opened their diapers — to find a scoop of Rocky Road ice cream. "Hands behind your backs!" shouted Carol. "And start eating!"

After the games came the presents. By this point, Jill was so traumatized she responded to each gift with a Stepford Wife smile and a simpering "thank you."

Just when she thought the worst was over, the other women began sharing stories of their own labor, delivery and postpartum experiences.

"52 hours of pure hell, then an emergency Caesarian."

"A huge episiotomy and I still tore like tissue paper in a tornado."

"Two suicide attempts in six months. Thank God they finally found an antidepressant that worked for me. The only side effect is total loss of interest in sex."

Finally, the horror was over. Everyone helped clean up, hugged Jill, and went on their merry way, each woman almost cleansed, as if Carol's living room had been a group confessional. Jill waddled her way out the door and into her mother-in-law's rented Chrysler.

"There," said June as they drove away. "That wasn't too bad, now was it, dear?"

Jill stared ahead and said flatly, "It was the worst moment of my life."

"Just you wait, dear," said June brightly. "Just you wait."

Bird

The first official sighting came at 6:38:25 Wednesday morning. As captured on the 911 recording, a woman's semi-hysterical voice hyperventilated, "There's a big blue bird in our backyard right now. And it's eating my flowers!"

Animal Control responded to the scene in time to see the gorgeous specimen lazily flap its wings and land on the roof of the house. The bird spread its plumage, looking like nothing so much as an exquisite blue lacquer Chinese fan.

"What is it?" said the homeowner, wrapping her housecoat around her.

"It's a peacock, lady."

The next sighting came outside Mapleton Elementary. All play in the playground stopped. Faces, child and adult alike, leaned out of every window. They followed the apparition as it flew up to perch on the tattered "Save Our School" banner. A visiting parent broke the silence with an awed whisper: "It's a sign."

Next the bird appeared on the roof of a small bungalow on the Naropa campus. Students gathered to take in its beauty and show off their own knowledge.

"The peacock is the national bird of India."

"Of course. It is also said to have a close connection to Lord Krishna."

"Obviously. But it is most venerated as the sacred vahana of Kartikeya."

149

The bird lifted one graceful leg, balancing effortlessly on its other leg. The students, without conscious thought, followed suit. They were still holding the posture long after the vahana had disappeared.

Pearl Street Mall received the next visitation. The peacock strutted confidently, head and tail high, cutting through the massed tourists, runaways, buskers and bad musicians. A crowd formed in its wake, a spontaneous parade jostling for a look at the proud parade master. The bird continued west, reaching Broadway where it swooped gracefully up onto a passing SKIP, leaving the parade to stare desolately after it.

The Bustop was in its mid-afternoon lull when the peacock appeared atop a stage-side table. It uttered an eerie cry, spread its full blue glory and stunned the dancers into mobility.

"He's staring straight at me," hissed one of the dancers.

"Like hell," said another, rotating her hips. "I think he wants a table dance with me."

At dusk two skateboarders looked up from their endless practicing just in time to see a grand blue blur descend from the sky and stride toward the food court entrance of the Crossroads Mall. The doors opened automatically and the peacock strutted inside.

Mall security sprang into action, attempting to corner the intruder. The bird ignored them, flitting from one vacant storefront to another, slipping effortlessly through the rolled-down metal gates. One security guard, in frustration, drew his weapon.

"What the hell are you doing?" yelled the mall's director of public relations. She produced a camera and focused on the bird. But before the camera could flash, the bird was gone, leaving not a single feather behind.

The last light of the day was slipping away as a crowd gathered on the eastern edge of Boulder. Drawn by some unexplainable inner drive, they stood silently, breaths held, staring up into the sky.

"There it is!" said someone. All heads swiveled to follow the graceful bird as it swooped down and landed right at their feet.

"They typically don't fly like that," said an ornithology professor from CU.

"According to Western science," sneered the Naropa students, all assuming the one-legged posture to honor the vahana.

The peacock flared its tail, mesmerizing the crowd. "I would kill for a gown that beautiful," whispered the Bustop dancer. "Or even one feather." She took a step forward, hand outstretched.

A volunteer from Peacock Rescue pulled the dancer back. "They cannot be caught; they must be lured." He pulled out a small bottle. "This is urine from a peahen in estrus."

"Put that piss away," said the PR lady. "I hearby designate that bird as the official Crossroads mascot."

"No way, he's our mascot," said the Mapleton parent.

The crowd surged forward, each one grasping for the bird. Elbows flew. Push came to shove. Each struggled to push him or herself forward while keeping the others back.

"He's getting away!" shouted a voice. All froze, turning to see the peacock fold its tail, spread its wings and leap into the air, a single ray of dying sunlight bathing it in red-golden glory as it disappeared, never to be seen again.

Except for two weeks later when it showed up with a peahen and two chicks. They looked around for a few days, then settled in Louisville where everyone knows you can get more nest for the money.

Driving pizza

Pete's financial straits were the result of a misunderstanding. He had called home to explain he needed a semester off to recharge his batteries, but somehow his father had acted like Pete was dropping out. "I swear I'm not dropping out," said Pete. "I just need time to find myself. It's only a semester off."

"Okay," said Dad. "I'll take a semester off, too — from sending checks."

This being the third year of the Bush economy, employment opportunities were, to say the least, limited. Pete could stuff burritos, clerk behind a Plexiglas shield or bag groceries. Instead he decided to drive pizza.

"You have any experience?" said the "Pop" of the little North Boulder Mom-and-Pop pizza shop Pete chose to apply at.

"Is that a problem?"

"Not necessarily. I got no problems with new guys — as long as they don't try to pull any crap. I run a small shop and an honest one. Everybody knows it. And everybody knows about this, too." Pop patted a bulge at his side. "44 magnum. Anyone comes in looking to steal from me, I won't be calling the cops until it's mopping up time."

The next night Pete met the other driver on duty, Jimbo. "You ever driven pizza before?" asked Jimbo. Pete shook his head. "Just you wait, my friend. I got lucky my very first delivery. Thirty-something blonde in a sheer

152

nightgown. Next thing I know she's doing things to me I ain't even seen on the Internet." Jimbo paused to relish the memory. "Anyway, here's the deal on the money. It sucks. The base is minimum wage. The per-trip is pathetic. Tips barely cover your gas. The only way to score at all is unde-liverables."

"Undeliverables?"

"Bad address or you get there and they swear they did-n't order a pizza. We're supposed to bring them back in and share them amongst ourselves. Instead, what you do is drive by an all-night place. Tell the guys on duty you got an extra pizza. Ask them if they want it for $10, $20, what-ever you think you can get. You keep the money. We all tell Pop you shared the pizza with us. Everybody's happy."

Before he knew it Pete was off on his first delivery. It took him longer than he'd expected, and instead of Kim Basinger, the door was opened by a couple of college kids who said "Thanks, dude," and stiffed him on a tip.

The next week went by in a blur. Pete quickly learned the vital skills of driving pizza: rolling stop signs, running red lights and staying off Foothills Parkway. On his third night, he got his first undeliverable. He slid to the curb in front of the address — a vacant lot. He checked the address again. No mistake. His heart pounded. He drove around and finally saw some guys working late in a bike repair shop. He stuck his head in, offered them the pizza (an extra-large with everything) and soon was on his way $10 richer.

Then he had an awful intuition. He pulled the delivery slip out of his pocket. As with all slips, there was the cus-tomer's phone number along the bottom. Pete drove to the nearest pay phone and dialed the number.

"Hello?"

"You ordered a pizza?"

"Is there a problem?"

"I just need to check the address."

The customer gave Pete the address, which was exactly one digit off from the one on the slip. Pete almost threw up right then and there. He drove around for 20 minutes, then returned to the shop. Not knowing what he was going to say, he walked up to Pop.

"I made a mistake," said Pete. Pop looked at him. "I was taking the pizza up the front steps — and it fell right out of the box and upside down in the shrubbery." He couldn't believe the words flowing out of his mouth "It was a total mess. I promised the customers I'd rush them out another one."

Pop stared silently, his eyes boring into Pete's. Pete didn't flinch, sticking with his story as if his life depended on it. Glancing at the bulge on Pop's hip, he realized it just might at that.

"What the hell," said Pop finally. "Everyone gets one mistake. Have kitchen make you up another extra-deluxe and tell the customer it's on the house."

Three hours later Pete's shift was over and he was driving home. His heart still beat in his chest. He felt emotionally wrung-out and exhilarated at the same time. He had told the stupidest lie in his life to a paranoid with a gun — and he'd gotten away with it. He sensed the experience had changed him in some profound way. He felt a new sense of power. Power that could be used for good or for evil.

Well, he had wanted to find himself. Now, by God, he had. He decided to call home the next day and tell his dad he was ready to start school again. With a new major.

Political Science.

Final week

Jill gave one final agonizing push and felt something slide out of her. She lifted her head to look down between her legs. There staring blandly up at her was George W. Bush's full-sized head. It was attached to an infant's body, all wrinkled and wet and red.

"Isn't he cute!" said one of the nurses.

Little W squeezed his face up and wailed, "I want a tax cut! I want a tax cut!"

Jill screamed, pushing the monster away and scrambling backwards off the operating table.

She landed on the floor, bruising her tailbone — and waking up. She blinked, looking around at the familiar environs of her bedroom. She felt her belly. Still swollen. She rubbed her ass. Definitely bruised. She pulled herself up onto her knees and shook the bed.

"Tom," she said sharply. "Wake up!"

Tom, of course, was already awake. Who could sleep with Jill's constant thrashing and sighing and 400 trips to the bathroom every night? He had begun to harbor fantasies of grabbing her belly in the middle of the night and just squeezing the kid out right then and there. He might have done it, too, if not for fear of what would come next.

Fatherhood.

"I'm coming," he said to Jill. He walked around and helped her get back up and onto the bed.

Jill adjusted herself in the bed and considered giving a sarcastic "thank you" to Tom. But she decided she had been so incredibly miserable this last week that he deserved to feel miserable and unappreciated, too. After all, without his "contribution" she wouldn't be in this state. Hell, she would be up in the mountains somewhere, lying out under the stars, enjoying the wind playing across her young, trim, un-varicosed body.

Tom got back into bed. He considered saying "you're welcome," but decided discretion was the better part of surviving the fortieth week. In his mind he ticked off the hours remaining until the official due date. Of course the due date was nothing but a guess on the doctor's part, but lately Tom had found himself clinging to it like a middle-school kid counting down the days to summer vacation.

Only, of course, the delivery date wouldn't be the beginning of anything like a summer vacation. In fact, there was every possibility he would look back to this very night as a golden moment in the "before" segment of his life. Because God knew, and everyone else had hinted, that life in the "after" segment would be different in huge and inexplicable ways. In fact, during last week's counseling session with Dr. Julie, she'd advised Tom and Julie to "cherish the short time they had left as a twosome."

Tom tried to lean back into his pillow and let himself cherish the moment — only to feel the bed shift as Jill pushed herself up and out and toward the bathroom.

Julie pulled up her nightgown, staring down at the flesh-tone super-sized beach ball that used to be her waistline. She squatted on the toilet and thought back to all the pregnant women she'd attended to in her nursing career. What a pain in the ass she'd considered them to be: whining and moaning about their condition as if they were overgrown versions of the babies they were carrying. Maybe her own third trimester was karmic punishment for every judgmental thought, every disapproving look, every short-tempered comment.

She rested her face in her hands, trying to decide whether to go back to bed or not. She couldn't bear another replay of the W dream again. The only thing worse was the one where Keanu Reeves popped out in black duster and shades, launched himself in a slow-motion back flip and kicked everyone's head in — including Jill's.

Tom waited for Jill to return, trying to decide if he should stay in bed or slip out and try to grab a few hours on the couch. Before he could make up his mind, the door opened and Jill hobbled back in. He lay unmoving as she plunked herself on the bed, squirmed into position, arranged the covers around her and sighed loud enough to wake everyone in Boulder.

Tom felt another, softer rustling and then the touch of Jill's hand on his. He let his fingers slip into hers. So quietly he had to strain his ears, she said words he had been longing to hear:

"After this one, never again."

He squeezed her hand tenderly and lovingly.

"Deal."

The House

She sat where she had always sat, looking out at a world that had changed much in 76 years. Her gaze was veiled now to discourage the morbid, hungry eyes that had gradually fallen in number but never totally disappeared. She met their stares, as she always had, with an impassive face that refused to even acknowledge their existence.

But now she was to be in the public eye once more. Her name was in the news. Her value was public knowledge. Her shame was bandied about in tones both righteous and lurid. And those with $1,600,000 to spend were welcomed inside to gawk at her most private places.

"As you can see, the house has been extensively renovated." The agent led the couple across the hardwood floors, their footsteps echoing in the emptiness. "The formal dining room is this way. Just beyond is the chef's kitchen with butler's pantry."

She focused her attention inward to study the intruders. Middle-aged. Money. An air of privilege just short of arrogance. She was not unfamiliar with the type. They followed the agent up the stairs.

"Wait 'til you see the master suite. It occupies the entire top floor and offers the most amazing mountain views."

They stood, looking around at the spacious rooms, their eyes taking in the details, while at the same time carefully concealing their thoughts.

"There's a finished basement," said the agent, the tilt of his body suggesting they follow him back down the stairs. The woman blanched and spoke up for the first time. "I'd rather not, if you don't mind. In fact, it's all very nice, but I don't think it's for us."

Her husband nodded, though there was the slightest suggestion of disappointment at not completing the tour. He recovered quickly, and she felt certain neither the wife nor the agent had caught sight of it.

The trio filed gracefully down the stairs, not speaking. At the entrance, the couple turned to give one last look. Their eyes were wider than they realized, as if following some unconscious desire to commit the scene to memory.

They left, and she was alone again with her secret.

The next day brought another agent with another couple, younger than the first. She knew right away something wasn't right about these two. Their clothing and their air pretended to money but didn't quite manage to pull it off. She could tell the agent was uneasy and at the same time unready to risk challenging what might after all prove to be legitimate clients.

"This is the dining room, right?" said the young man, leading the way. "And the kitchen. Just as I thought, it opens on the rear spiral staircase."

The young woman tried to signal her partner to cool his enthusiasm, but he didn't notice. He disappeared down the stairs. The young woman shrugged at the agent who gave her a hard look before disappearing down the stairs himself.

At the bottom, the young man was pacing off steps, following an inner map until he stood before a plain white wall. The agent caught up with him just as he placed his hands on the wall.

"It was behind here," he whispered. "They've bricked it over."

"Sir," said the agent. "This showing is over. Please leave now before I call the police."

"Not yet. I've waited so long. I'm a sensitive. Just give me fifteen minutes and I know I can make contact."

She couldn't help but laugh to herself at his words. He froze, cocking his head as if he could, in fact, hear her laughter.

The agent took the opportunity to dial 911. Soon the police arrived to escort the intruders out. It wasn't the first time she'd played host to the police, of course. She retained fond feelings for the earlier ones, the pawns who'd never stood a chance in the face of money and influence.

But wasn't that what made her timeless? Death is all too common. Murder, as well. No one notes for long the simple stories of rage, impulse, remorse, punishment. It was money and influence and the power to cloud the truth that made for a timeless story. And as the years passed, the unspeakable violation and killing of a child would somehow become more and more like a fiction, a made-up drama, unreal and distant.

And passers-by would feel an almost pleasant shiver as they whispered to one another, "That's it, isn't it? That's The House."

What a year!

5:25 AM Jill shook Tom's shoulder. "Mbwahhh," he said (or something to that effect). She shook him again, moaning as another contraction overtook her. Tom instinctively reached over to Jill's side of the bed.

It was empty.

Tom shot upright, staring panicked at the place where his pregnant and helpless wife was supposed to be. Jill calmly tapped his shoulder from behind. His head whipped around to find her standing, dressed, her hair freshly cleaned, her packed bag on the floor beside her.

She winced and glanced at her watch. "Three minutes apart. Intense and regular. If we leave right now, we should have just enough time to get there."

6:32 AM Crystal was power-walking up the steep trail behind NOAA when she spied the mysterious figure at the edge of the trail. Something about the tilt of his head told Crystal he was not your usual emotionally-sensitive, in-touch-with-his-inner-feminine Boulder male. Unconsciously she pulled back her shoulders and picked up her pace. She took a few yoga breaths to help recover her non-attachment.

Jake scoped the blonde from behind his shades. He approved of the fact her body was gently rounded and feminine. Not like the muscular specimens, both male and female, who ran past in their spandex uniforms. They had long puzzled Jake until he had realized they were secret U.N. shock troops headquartered here in Boulder awaiting the order to confiscate America's guns and turn it into a slave state of the

One-World Government.

She glanced casually his way and hazarded a small smile. He seemed taken aback. She mentally kicked herself. Then he smiled and said, "Hello."

"Beautiful view," she said.

"Yes, it is," he said, looking her up and down. She blushed. What kind of tramp was she turning into? As for Jake, he couldn't believe he'd said it either. What the hell was he doing fraternizing with the enemy? He was in Boulder on an undercover assignment from the Brigade Commander himself. Still, it could be a tactical advantage to recruit a local. He stepped onto the trail beside her, matching her pace. "So, what exactly do you think they do in all that space?" He pointed down.

"Don't laugh, but sometimes I think the whole thing's a secret alien processing center. They're real, you know."

"Tell me about it. Crawling across our borders, stealing our resources, corrupting our morals."

"Or maybe they're beings of light and healing energy."

He looked at her as if she had spoken in an alien tongue herself.

"All I know is," she continued, "the government's hiding the truth from us."

"Yes, yes," he said, excited she got at least part of it.

"Sometimes I think we'd all be better off if there were no governments and we were all free to follow our own hearts."

His heart soared. He didn't trust his voice to tell her he believed exactly the same thing. He shyly took her hand. She shyly let him and they continued on their path, side by side.

A perfect Boulder couple.

6:34 AM Tom drove hard, taking Martin to Baseline to Broadway to the Hospital. Along the way, they passed the new Mexican restaurant in the building where the old Italian restaurant had failed after some other restaurant had failed before it. Just what Boulder needed: more oversized burritos and cheap Margaritas.

"Two minutes apart," said Jill.

Tom blew through a yellow light, taking the turn onto Broadway on two wheels. He was glad for the paucity of students. Usually they turned Broadway into a human obstacle course. It reminded Tom of a long-ago family vacation. They had been driving when all of a sudden they came upon thousands and thousands of frogs hopping across the road. Tom's dad slowed way down, but still the thumps continued, the green faces landing on the windshield to peer accusingly inside. Idly, Tom wondered if a student would wear the same look of half-confusion/half-accusation as he or she slid down the windshield and off the front of the car.

"Ow!" moaned Jill.

Tom mashed the accelerator.

8:58 AM The Internet had the story first, followed shortly by the cable "news" shows. An inner member of the Bush circle had come forth to admit that the President and his men had known all along that there were no WMDs in Iraq. Within an hour a press conference was called. The President huffed and dithered and finally broke down in tears and said yes, yes, it was all true. Everything the "liberals" had been saying about him all along.

Before noon the House voted to impeach and the Senate to convict. Then the Justice Department filed charged of treason. Bush was shipped to Guantanamo in irons, tears streaming down his broken face. A national dragnet swept up every member of the radical right cabal (including 51% of Congress) and sent them down to Guantanamo to join their fallen leader.

Al Gore was offered the job he had rightly won. He turned it down. Ralph Nader volunteered to step in, but he was placed in irons and shipped to Guantanamo just for poetic justice.

Then the kettle whistled in the kitchen.

Dorothy looked up from her daydream, sighing. She made

tea, then returned to the letter she was writing to the editor. She finished another couple of sentences before resting her chin on her hand and falling back into reverie.

Dick Cheney sweated in the cage next to Bush's. Again, he tried to rouse his former puppet. "This is no time to go soft, George," he hissed. "We need to escape and regroup. Corporations are counting on us. Rich white men. Military contractors. Religious nutcases. We can't let them down."

"Oh, shut up," said Bush. "Or I'll tell them where you hid all those Haliburton profits."

11:29 AM "Gaia!" shouted Astrid, searching the trail ahead of her.

"Come find me!" called Gaia (if only in Astrid's mind's ear). What else could you expect from the spirit of a Goddess living in the body of a border collie? Astrid kept her eyes open for a ranger. The last thing she needed was another ticket for "non-voice-and-sight-control." As if humans had the right to "control" any other living creature.

O, the unbearable hubris of it all!

Astrid heard something off to her right, then Gaia burst onto the trail, a brown lump clenched in her teeth. For a moment, deep in the catacombs of Astrid's brain, an image thrust itself up into her consciousness. An image of Gaia, the all-loving, embodiment of Mother Earth herself, crushing a tiny wriggling prairie dog in her jaws and gulping it down.

At the time this actually happened, Astrid's entire universe of total love, sacred nature and the tender interconnectedness of all beings (save the humans who were too dumb and greedy to even deserve to be called a part of nature) had crumbled right before her eyes. It was as if she herself were dying. Then the executive part of her brain snatched up the image/memory and flung it down into the catacombs with the rest of the repressed and forbidden.

Luckily, this time no such mental gymnastics would be required. The brown lump slipped out of Gaia's jaws. Astrid saw it was nothing but a short, thick, bark-covered stick.

Stick in mouth, Gaia and Astrid continued their hike. Astrid particularly loved this part of the Mesa Trail. The trees shaded them from the sun — and other people. They could pretend they alone walked this sacred earth.

A flash of tan caught Astrid's eye. She glanced up at the flank of a deer on the rocks a couple hundred feet above them. She glanced immediately down to make sure Gaia hadn't caught the scent and was even now preparing to lunge up and take off after the deer. Fortunately, Gaia seemed content to continue her parade master duties. When Astrid glanced back up, her eyes were confused. The flank and haunches she had caught glimpse of were indeed tan. But their proportions seemed off for a deer.

It wasn't a deer. It was a mountain lion. And it was staring straight into Astrid's eyes. Astrid was frozen. She couldn't pull her eyes away. A primitive part of her brain calculated the distance between them and announced the lion, if it wanted to, could reach her in three seconds. Other primitive parts chimed in and for the fist time in her life Astrid felt like prey.

She saw the incredible, fierce beauty of the beast, shaped by nature to run down and devour helpless creatures just like Astrid. In that frozen moment, Astrid's only thought was, "Someone, please kill it."

The lion turned its noble head, no longer interested in Astrid. Astrid sprang from her frozen position and ran off down the trail, her brain already obscuring the memory.

Lea, from her rocky perch, watched the human run away in panic. Please. Too skinny for her taste, and probably bitter. No, give Lea a young, plump jogger any day.

"Yum," thought Lea.

1:44 PM "Push!" cried Tom. It had been a long ordeal but the moment was at hand.

"Crowning," said the OB from down between Jill's knees. "Give us one more push."

Jill pushed and felt the head slide out. A small flurry of activity from the OB and nurses and more pushing on Jill's part, and it was done. Jill waited, her breath still, for what seemed like forever. Then she heard a tiny lusty cry. She slumped back down,

"It's a boy!" said the OB, lifting a squishy red shape up for all to see. The next thing Jill knew he was lying on her chest, still crying, looking up at her. So beautiful. So precious. So significant. How had she survived 34 empty, meaningless years without these tiny precious eyes looking into hers?

"Smile for the video," said Tom, leaning in close.

Jill ignored him, focussing all her attention on her finally-arrived reason for living.

4:10 PM "I want to go swimming."

"I'd take you if I could, honey bunch, but I'm up to my ass in paperwork and — " Jeff looked up to find Linda glaring at him from the doorway of the home office.

"Daddy said ass!" giggled Claire.

"And Daddy is putting down his work right now and taking you to the new North Boulder Rec Center pool."

On the way there, Claire chattered incessantly. "What's that sign say?" and "Are we there?" and "Let's sing Old McDonald Had a Farm!" Jeff did his best to play along while the majority of his brain was going over all the work he was snowed under. Well, he'd slipped his briefcase in the back seat while Linda was busy helping Claire get ready. Maybe now he could find a poolside chair and work — while, of course, keeping an eye on Claire.

Inside the Rec Center, they dressed in one of the family dressing rooms. Claire chattered and pretended everything was a race. "Don't take off your shoes yet." He complied and watched her take off her shoes then jump up and down saying, "I win! I win! Nanny nanny boo boo!" Jeff got his trunks on (covering himself with a towel to keep his private parts private). His bladder felt just a bit full, but there was no way he could use the toilet in the changing room without showing Claire more than he and Linda had decided was good for her at this age.

A quick shower and they were into the pool area. Or as Jeff saw immediately, "The Ninth Pit of Hell." Gushing water. Spraying water. Countless hellions shrieking and splashing. And as if the normal kid chaos wasn't enough, an assortment of Rube Goldberg devices, each one designed to splash and spray any person stupid enough to be in the pool. Which, of course, did not include Jeff. He found a chair beside the pool and opened the briefcase.

It was empty — except for a single post-it note. "Nice try," it said. "Play with your daughter."

Sighing, Jeff waded into the pool. It wasn't exactly freezing, but it was still chilly to his skin. When he finally reached Claire, she screamed with joy. He bent and hugged her waterlogged, wriggling body. It was deeper here, almost three feet. He settled near the edge, close to Claire.

She was overjoyed to have Daddy watching her. She showed off everything she could do. She ran through the jetting spouts. She swung on the cord and dumped water on her head. She went down the slide over and over again. Jeff couldn't help but smile. She was so happy. And every so often she'd splash over to press her dripping head to his chest and say, "I love you, Daddy!"

After about an hour, Jeff was thinking about rounding up Claire. The only problem was that his bladder was by now full to bursting. He could try to hold it 'til they got home. Impossible. He could run into the locker rooms and leave Claire out of his sight for a few minutes. Unacceptable. He could bring her into the changing room with him, make her swear to not peek at Daddy peeing. Unlikely. There was only one other option. Jeff checked and rechecked his logic, each time coming to the same conclusion.

So he gave in to the inevitable and for the first time in

weeks actually felt his body relax and go with the flow.

It felt good.

Warmed up the water, too.

5:41 PM Todd rushed around the apartment, making sure everything was just so — from the scented candles to the huge centerpiece of florally-arranged red leaf lettuce. (Private joke.) He took a quick shower and slipped on the satin pants and safari jacket outfit he had saved up three months for. One quick spray of Romance and he was ready.

And not a second too early. He heard Mark's key in the lock. Todd waited breathlessly in the bedroom, listening for Mark's reaction.

He heard nothing.

After two minutes, he walked into the living room to find Mark in front of the TV. "Hey," said Mark, giving Todd the barest of glances before returning his attention to the screen.

Todd was stunned. His face ached as if Mark had actually slapped him. "Turn that piece of shit off this minute!"

With a melodramatic sigh, Mark turned off the TV. "What did I do now?"

It was like spraying gasoline on a fire. "What did you do?," screamed Tom. "Are you blind, deaf and dumb? Are you even aware that this is our sixth month anniversary of moving in together? Or is your narcissism so advanced you truly cannot see anyone else? Or are you seeing someone else? Who is it? Is it Steve? Tell me it's not Steve! That little red-haired hussy!"

Just as Todd was about to shift the tirade into second gear, he heard a noise from outside. He turned toward the balcony. And found it full of their friends. Wearing party hats, holding presents and covering their mouths to keep from laughing out loud. Right in front, behind the red light of a video camera, was Steve. He blew Todd a kiss.

Later that evening, during a lull in the festivities, Todd pulled Mark down onto his lap. "You terrible sneak," he whispered. "I wanted it to be just the two of us tonight."

"It will be, sweetheart," Mark laughed lasciviously. "But first — " He raised his champagne flute. "Thank all of you, our dear and queer friends, for being here to celebrate this milestone with us. I wish for each and every one of you the love I've found with this wonderful man." He grabbed Todd in a deep, passionate kiss. Everyone hooted and whistled and applauded as Todd blushed redder and redder.

Until he was exactly the same shade of red as the lettuce in the centerpiece.

11:58 PM Tom took the baby from Jill's arms and hugged him to his chest. Instead of taking little Will back to the nursery, he carried his son over the big open window.

Below them lay that town so impossible to truly grasp while so easy to caricature. Where liberals lay down next to libertarians. Where real estate and chakras competed for the town's heart. Where runaways shared the mall with rich tourists who could easily have been their parents. Where cute little thunderheads crept over the mountain tops every afternoon to drizzle, storm, thunder and light up the deep, rich sky. Where polite brown people worked tirelessly and invisibly to keep everything going. Where laid-off high tech workers bunked three or four to an apartment while their laid-off managers hunkered down in Devil's Thumb, praying to make the next month's mortgage payment. Where everyone hunkered down inside the green Open Space doughnut to ride out the devastation of the Bush years. Where water rights and no-spray policies and traffic mitigation and school closings and slumping sales taxes and wind energy and Shakespeare and tubing and blading and gliding and prairie dogs and so much more was waiting for a tiny baby boy to grow up and grab hold of the whole foolish, idealistic, hypocritical, beautiful mess as his birthright.

"Welcome to Boulder," Tom whispered.